Give Me Something I Can Feel

A romance by:
B. Love

D1403326

www.authorblove.com

This is a work of fiction. Names, characters, places and incidents either are products of the author's imagination or are used fictitiously. Any resemblance to actual events or locales or persons, living or dead, is entirely coincidental.

For information about bulk purchases, please contact B. Love via email – authorblove@gmail.com

Hey!

Thanks so much for reading!

Very quickly I wanted to let you know about my giveaway! I am giving away four fire tablets four days after the release of this book. Details on how to enter and win will be at the end!

Also, if you enjoy reading about Knight and Charlie, I'd appreciate it if you left a review and recommended this book to your friends!

All my best to you,

B. Love

His Prologue

Knight rushed through the emergency room. All eyes were on him – on the wide eyed man whose clothes were drenched with rain – but his eyes were on the front desk attendant. Police followed behind Knight, trying and failing to secure him. Speeding ticket be damned. Right now, his only concern was his mother. He'd deal with everything else later.

Trembling hands grabbed the glass that separated him from the attendant, and Knight pulled it apart. His temporary stillness made it easy for the police that were following him to restrain him.

"Get the fuck off of me!" Knight roared as he fought against the four arms that were restraining him.

Gasps, whispers, and screams poured from all over the waiting room.

"Please, sir, remain calm. I do not want to have to tase you," one of the officers warned.

Knight's head went to the left, and his eyes locked with the attendant.

"Can you please tell me what room my mother is in? Angela Carver."

The attendant nodded quickly and pecked away at her computer. Handcuffs were placed on Knight's wrists, then he was lifted to his feet and read his rights.

"She's in room 216," the attendant pointed to a set of double doors to the right of her. "Go straight through and turn right."

Knight nodded and looked at the police that was standing behind him.

"I don't mind going to jail for whatever y'all are trying to charge me with. Just let me see my mother before I go. That's the only reason I was speeding and didn't stop. I needed to get to her. Please, let me see her before you take me."

The officers looked from one to the other, agreeing silently. Knight was led behind those double doors, and each step he took seemed to have weakened him. His mother had struggled with diabetes for years. It didn't matter how much they tried to make her eat right and take better care of herself, she didn't take her illness seriously. As most people don't.

Angela continued to neglect her health.

And now... the stroke that may or may not take her life was making her pay for it.

Knight saw his father, Princeton, standing outside of room 216 speaking with his mother's doctor. Princeton's eyes were lowered towards the ground, but the closer Knight got the higher his father's eyes went. They went from Knight's shoes to his legs. They lingered at his chest for a while. Then landed on his eyes. And as soon as they did... Knight fell to his knees and hung his head.

The officers tried to lift him up, but he was too heavy. Not physically but emotionally. The look on his father's face told him all that he needed to know about his mother's condition.

"Why is my son in handcuffs?" Princeton asked as he kneeled before Knight and grabbed his face to look into his eyes.

"We arrested him for speeding, evading arrest, and assaulting a police officer but..." the officer that cuffed him earlier removed them. "We're just gonna... let it go this time."

The officers helped Knight stand, and they both patted him on his back before walking away. Knight inhaled deeply and looked past Princeton towards his mother's room.

"What happened, Pops?"

"What didn't happen?" the light laugh that fell from Princeton's lips in no way matched the tears in his eyes. "Kidneys are failing. She had a stroke. Stroke left her brain dead. She's falling apart, son. She's falling apart."

"But... that's... people live after having a stroke all the time. Dialysis for her kidneys... she can make it out of this like she makes it out of everything."

And by everything Knight meant his mother's battle with her sight weakening. High blood pressure. Nerve problems. Consistent swelling in her ankles and feet, and skin infections and sores.

"It's not that simple, Knight. She's... she doesn't want to do the dialysis, and we can't make her."

"The fuck you mean we can't make her? You're her husband! She has kids! She can't just give up! Make her ass go on a diet and start eating right, but you can't kill her!"

"*Enough!* I get that you're upset, but you will *not* disrespect me. You're right; I am her husband, and I'm going to respect her wishes. I'm not going to be selfish and keep her here just to suffer and appease us. If she wants to let things happen naturally that's what we're going to do," Knight tried to walk away, but Princeton grabbed his arm and pulled him closer. "And we're going to support her no matter what happens."

Knight looked from his father to his mother's room. His fingers grazed the top of his head as he sighed deeply. With slumped shoulders he nodded. Princeton released his arm and wrapped his arm around Knight's shoulder. Slowly, he led Knight towards Angela's room.

"She's on life support. We're going to take her off. We just wanted to give you time to get here and say goodbye just in case she isn't strong enough to fight."

Knight briefly hesitated. Measuring the space between him and room 216. He looked back towards the double doors. As if simply running out of them and hopping back in his car and returning to his basketball game could make all of this a horrible nightmare.

The closer he got to her room, the closer the walls wrapped around him. By the time he finally made it and saw her lying atop her bed he'd swear the walls were crushing him at the sides. Flattening him. Forcing him to feel nothing but pain. Discomfort. Tightness.

The stillness made her look peaceful. More peaceful than she had looked the past few times he'd seen her. That may have been a good thing.

Knight looked over at his younger sister, Harlem, as she sat in the corner. Legs pulled up in her chair. Elbows on her knees. Eyes focused intently on her mother. Like she was afraid that if she looked away...

"Mr. Carver, can I speak with you outside?"

Knight looked towards the door where the voice came from. Princeton nodded and went outside to speak with Angela's doctor. With an odd and unfamiliar tinge of disappointment, Knight walked over to his mother and ran his finger across her cheek – pulling back immediately at the feel of her cold skin.

Blinded by tears that choked his voice, Knight muttered, "Why won't you fight?" as he lowered his forehead to hers. "Why are you giving up on us?"

And then he remembered... she wouldn't be able to answer him.

"Knight, it's time."

Knight ran his fingers through his mother's hair at the sound of his father's voice. Refusing to stay and watch her leave, he walked over to Harlem and kissed her cheek before walking out of the room abruptly.

Her Prologue

"She's just… she's just a little girl. There must be *something* you can do."

Chelsey's shaking hands grabbed the top of Doctor Berry's lab coat. Before he could try to pull her away, her husband, William, was grabbing her by her waist and putting space between her and the doctor.

"I'm sorry, Mrs. White, but there's nothing else we can do at this point. Your daughter's heart is failing. It's enlarged and it's tired. We've tried every possible medicine. Every surgery. Every treatment. There's nothing else we can do. If we don't have a closely matched donor… there's just nothing else that we can do. I'm sorry."

Doctor Berry walked away, and William deemed it safe to release his wife. Chelsey began to pace in front of Charlie's room as she shook her head. Weighed down with the feeling of failing her daughter. Her baby daughter. As Charlie's mother, Chelsey thought it was her responsibility to do all she could to keep her alive and well.

Chelsey brought her into this world, and she refused to allow anything to take her out this young.

"If we can't find a donor I'm going to give her my heart, William," Chelsey's voice was calm. A little too calm for William. Like she'd been considering this for a while. That would make sense. Charlie had been having heart issues for years. At 19, there was no question in William's mind about how many scenarios Chelsey had come up with to keep her daughter here. "I'm not going to just stand out here and allow her to just… *die*. For her heart to just… stop. No. If a donor is the problem… I'll donate mine."

William sighed and ran his hands over his face.

"Chels, it's not that simple, hon. You have to be a good, close match. You're not. If you were we'd know. And even if you were a match, how do you think she'd feel if she woke up and you were gone?"

"I don't care how she'd feel. Feelings will change. She'd be alive. That's all that matters to me."

There was no point in arguing with her when she got like this, so William pulled her into his arms and held her close instead.

"She's my baby, William. My baby."

William kissed the top of Chelsey's head and sighed deeply.

"I know, hon. I know."

"Mom, Dad," Rodney, Charlie's older brother called as he marched down the hallway towards them.

Charlie's older sister, Veronica, was right behind him. And her best friend, Deja, was behind her. Chelsey pulled herself from William's grip at the sight of her children. Now, she had to be strong for them. Rodney fell into her arms as Veronica hugged her father. Deja leaned against the wall as she stared at Charlie's door absently.

"What are they saying?" Veronica inquired.

Chelsey looked at William to answer as she grabbed Veronica's hand.

"Her heart is extremely enlarged. Because of that her body is retaining fluid. Her lungs are congested. They have her on a breathing machine, and they're trying to slow her heart palpitations down, but none of the medicine is working."

"Did they try water? That worked last time," Deja offered – her eyes still trained on the door.

"Yes. No change. And they don't want to give her too many IV's because she's already swelling from the fluid. Dr. Berry is saying that besides a donor there's nothing else that they can do."

"Nothing else they can do?" Rodney repeated. "So what? They're just going to let my baby sister die? The fuck type of shit is that? I'll give her my heart."

Chelsey smiled and lowered her head as tears began to fall.

"You know just like your mother knows that's not how it works, Rod. If it was that easy I'd be beside her giving her mine."

"Can I talk to her?" Deja interjected.

"Just for a little while. She's out of breath and exhausted. She doesn't need to overwork herself. Make sure she keeps the mask on," William instructed.

Deja nodded and walked into Charlie's room. She kept the door open – truthfully, scared to be alone with her. Standing at the foot of Charlie's bed, Deja looked down at her as she ran her thumb across Charlie's ankle softly.

Charlie's eyebrows wrinkled, and her eyes fluttered open weakly. Her cheeks raised as she smiled at the sight of Deja. Deja returned the smile as tears filled her eyes.

"Don't try to talk. I just... wanted to tell you that I was here and I love you. All of your family is outside."

Charlie nodded as a tear slid down her cheek. Deja made her way to Charlie's side. Grabbing her left hand, Deja wiped the tear away.

"What's wrong, Charlie?"

Charlie shook her head as she placed her free hand on top of her heart. Her mouth opened, but she closed it. Deja pulled the mask up slightly so Charlie could speak.

"It hurts."

Deja put the mask back down before she replied.

"It hurts? Your heart?"

Charlie nodded as another tear fell. In all the years Deja had known her, she'd never seen her cry over her condition. Deja looked from Charlie to the outside of the room where her family stood. She tried to walk away to get her parents, but Charlie put all of her strength into holding Deja's hand.

"I was just going to get your parents."

Charlie shook her head. Deja lifted the mask.

"Don't. I've worried them enough. Just... pray for me."

Deja nodded and inhaled deeply as her lips trembled. She rubbed her lips together and looked down at Charlie. Her heart was beating close to 250 times a minute, yet the rise and fall of her chest was painstakingly slow. But it was hard. She could literally see Charlie's heart beating.

Charlie closed her eyes. Deja did the same.

"Gracious and eternal God..." Deja paused and inhaled deeply again as she fought back tears. "Thank you for You. For the Holy Trinity. For Jesus – whose stripes have already secured Charlie's healing. For Your Holy Spirit – who gives us Your strength. Your peace. God, I'm not sure what you have in store for Charlie, but..." the tears she'd been holding in finally began to fall. "But if you could just... take her pain away. Be it here or there... I just want my best friend's pain to be over. In Jesus name I pray am–"

Deja's eyes bolted open at the sound of Charlie's machine flat lining.

"Charlie..." she nudged an unresponsive Charlie on the shoulder as her family rushed into her room. "Charlie!"

"What happened?" Chelsey grabbed Charlie's hand as Deja backed away. "What happened, Deja? Rodney, get her doctor!"

"I was just praying for her... then the machine started..."

Deja's head shook as she continued to back away from Charlie. Doctor Berry sprinted into the room and took Chelsey's place at Charlie's side as three other doctors followed behind him.

"We need the room clear. Everyone out."

Deja watched as Charlie was unhooked and rolled out of the room. Still unresponsive. Everyone followed behind as Charlie was rolled out. Except Deja. She stayed behind and fell to her knees.

"OK, I lied – I don't want her pain to be over. Not if it means she has to die. Please, don't take her away from me. From us. Please."

10 years later...

≥ KNIGHT ≤

Sinead was beating on my hotel room door like she didn't have any common sense. I don't know why she thought randomly popping up at my hotel would make me talk to her. I guess she thought since I was back in her hometown of Cleveland that this was her best chance of getting me to talk to her.

Wrong.

When I ended things with a woman... I ended things with a woman.

It didn't matter what she said or did to try to get me back; when I made up my mind to call things off that was it.

To be honest, I can't even come up with a reason why Sinead was taking losing me so hard anyway. We weren't in a committed relationship. I wasn't a big texter and phone talker, so we hardly communicated. For the most part, I'd hit her up when I was in town or I'd fly her to wherever my job had me when I wanted female companionship.

As a sports announcer for the Memphis Grizzlies, I was on the road more than I was ever home. My lifestyle didn't leave room for commitment and consistency. I made that perfectly clear to Sinead, but she allowed herself to go and fall for me anyway. Now she expected me to pick her up when I'd told her from the jump that I wouldn't.

I told her that I was no good.

No good for her at least.

I told her that all I could offer her was sex.

Not even consistent sex.

As usual, she thought she would be able to use her body to secure my heart... and as usual... she was wrong.

Women could spare themselves so much pain if they actually listened to what a man said. If they actually took the time to ask him from the jump what his intentions were. If a man doesn't want commitment, there's nothing you can do to make him commit to you but show him what he has in you. What he has in you has to be something different from all the other women he could be with. Having sex with him or telling him you're cool with just kicking it knowing damn well you want a committed relationship is not the way to go about it. He can kick it and have sex with any woman.

If you really want to stand out... be honest and upfront from the jump about what you want and make *him* meet *your* demands. Don't settle for less than what you want and deserve. Don't settle for sex and friendship with benefits if you want more, because once you put yourself in that friend position... you'll have the hardest time getting him to see you as more.

Men love to chase. We take pride in working for our woman. In our treasure. If he doesn't want to work for you, you're not his treasure. If you're not his treasure, you will never have his heart. You'll never be the one he fights to keep.

So yea, after I called things off with Sinead a week ago it didn't cross my mind that she'd track me down tonight, but I should have expected that. She was the kind of woman that felt like because she was beautiful and had a nice body she could have any man she wanted. And when a man that she wanted didn't want her that was a kick to her ego. Now she felt like she had a point to prove. She felt like she had to make me want her.

Wrong again.

I was aware of her beauty just like every other man that laid eyes on her... but it would take much, much more than a pretty face and curvy shape to secure my interest. When I decided to commit, which I don't see happening any time soon, it will be with a woman with substance. And Sinead was... shallow and empty.

Grabbing my phone off the dresser, I ignored Sinead's call and checked the time. I had thirty minutes to finish getting ready before I had to head to the arena. It was our last game of the season and it was on the road, so I wanted to give myself time to go and give the team a pep talk as well.

Sinead called again as she continued to bang on my door. As I placed her contact on my blocked list, my youngest sister Harlem called me. I had two. Harlem, who was 16, and Carmen, who was closer to my age at 25. Harlem was definitely an oopsie baby for my parents. They only planned on having two children. Carmen and I. I'm the oldest at 32, and Carmen was supposed to be the baby, but nine years later mama got pregnant with Harlem, and she's been my pride and joy ever since. Both of my sisters are, but Harlem holds a special place in both me and Carmen's heart because she was so young when mama died.

"Hey, sweetheart," I answered as I sat in the chair that was in the dining area of my room. My mood was instantly calmed and brightened by her calling, and she hadn't even said anything yet. "What's up?"

"Boo… what is that noise in the background?"

My eyes shifted towards the door as I sighed.

"Nothing. What's up, Harlem?"

"You got another crazy one don't you? I told you about messing with all those different women, Knight. You need to stop. I don't have time to be catching a flight cause one of them hopping on some *Thin Line Between Love and Hate* shit."

"Watch your mouth. And what you know about that movie? You weren't even born when it came out, girl."

"So! I watch *Martin* all the time and I watched all his movies!"

"What do you want, sweetheart? I need to finish getting ready so I can head to the arena."

She blew a loud breath into the phone and the beating of my heart picked up.

"Knight…" Harlem paused and exhaled loudly again. "I have to tell you something."

"OK. What?"

"First, promise me that you won't get mad."

"I will not."

"Knight!"

I smiled and stood. Once I was at my bed I placed her call on speaker so I could finish getting dressed.

"Just tell me what you have to tell me. Don't make me make a promise I might not be able to keep."

"Fine…" another pause. "Daddy kicked me out. I've been staying with Princess and her family for the last week. When are you coming home?"

My shirt was tossed back onto the bed as I snatched my phone up.

"Pops kicked you out? For what? Why didn't you call me sooner?"

Their relationship was definitely strained. There was just… so much friction between them.

Pops had no experience raising a daughter on his own. When mama died Carmen was 15 and damn near taking care of herself by that point. Mama had had enough time to instill a taste of independence in her that she didn't have time to instill in Harlem. Carmen left Memphis for college and hadn't returned since. Every break she had she was flying Harlem out to Atlanta to spend time with her, but besides her, Harlem didn't really have any female influences.

The girlfriends my dad tried to bring around didn't last long because Harlem ran them all away, and our grandmothers were so old school everything they said to Harlem went in one ear and out of the other. Harlem rebelled. Period. She was a little troublemaker, and I was the only one that tried to take the time to break that shell.

"I didn't call because I knew off season was coming up and I was hoping you'd come home so I could stay with you."

Sitting on the edge of the bed, I switched the phone from my left ear to the right and massaged my left temple.

"Why did he kick you out, Harlem?"

This wasn't the first time she'd left the house. Most times it was after he'd tell her, "As long as you stay under my roof you'll abide by my rules. If you don't like my rules leave my house." It was always her choice to leave. I can't think of one time he'd ever forced her to.

"Cause," her voice was a lot softer than it was when she first called.

"Because what, Harlem?"

"I'm pregnant."

The fast pace at which my heart was beating stopped. Completely. It completely stopped beating. Then it plummeted. Fell so low it was like the weight of her words had literally detached it from the valves that were holding it. Fell so low I groaned. I was heartbroken. *Heartbroken.*

"What? Harlem…"

"I only have two years in school left, boo. I'm going to get a job now, and keep it while I'm in school. Then, when I turn 18 I'm going to move out and work a real fulltime job so I can take care of my baby. I just need you to let me stay until daddy lets me come back."

"No. You're not going to cancel college just because you're pregnant. You're not going to cut your dreams off just because of this baby. And you for damn sure aren't going to marry whoever the father is just because he got you pregnant. I refuse to let you ruin your life, Harlem. If pops doesn't want you to stay with him you can stay at my place. I'll take care of you and you take care of the baby. You're going to stay in school, graduate, and go to college just as you've always planned. Am I making myself clear?"

Her sniffles caught me off guard. Harlem was tough. She hardly ever cried.

"I hear you, Knight. Thank you."

18

"No thanks needed. I planned on going to Miami tomorrow, but I'll switch my flights out and head home. I'll pick you up from Princess's house then. And Harlem..."

"Yes?"

"We have a lot to talk about. You know that, right?"

"I know. I'll be prepared for your rant. I'm sure it won't be as bad as daddy's was."

"We'll talk about that too. I really have to go, though. I love you. I'll see you tomorrow."

"OK. I love you too."

I disconnected the call and just... sat there for a second. Completely tuned everything around me out. How did this shit happen? How was my baby about to have a baby? Didn't Carmen have the sex talk with her? Didn't I threaten her and the lil knuckleheads she brought around enough to avoid this?

True, I hadn't been home in about six months... but damn.

Shaking the guilt that was slowly starting to consume me off, I finished dressing and prayed that Sinead would be gone by the time I had to leave the hotel. I already wasn't in the mood for her mess, but now, I really didn't want to be bothered with her or anyone else.

We won the game and headed to the club to celebrate. Partying wasn't really my thing, but I wanted to celebrate with my team. It was always a good feeling to start and end the season with a win, so we had a lot to be proud of and celebrate.

Even with that in mind, I found myself sitting in the back of VIP next to a bucket of melted ice and unopened champagne. I'll be the first to admit, when mama died I was the first to pull away from my family. She was what held us together. She was our glue. So when she died... we just... unraveled. Carmen left for school. Pops shut down emotionally. Harlem started wilding out.

Over the years that's been fine with me. Well not fine, but I didn't see the need to try to pull my family back together. But now… all I wanted to do was go home, make Carmen bring her ass home, and get this shit together.

Deciding to flow with it, I pulled my phone out to send her a text.

911 at home. How soon can you get there?

Sliding my phone back into my pocket, I sat back in my seat and allowed my head to rest on the wall. My eyes scanned the VIP area I was in the back of, and when they landed on Sinead they stopped. Thankfully, she'd left by the time I had to leave the hotel, and I was hoping she'd come to her senses, but she obviously was just taking the time to regroup.

As soon as our eyes connected she started walking towards me. The vibrating of my phone pulled my attention away from her, so I pulled it out of my pocket and read Carmen's text.

Biggest little sis: I can come Friday after work. What's going on? Call me.

We'll talk about it when you get here. Don't worry yourself between now and Friday. Just get here when you can.

"Why haven't you been answering my phone calls, Knight? And I know you heard me outside of your hotel room. You're so predictable. You stay at the same hotel in the same room every time you come. I know you were in there."

I waited until the message said delivered before closing the thread out and putting my phone back in my pocket.

"Have a seat," I offered.

I didn't want any attention brought onto us. And the way she was hovering over me with one hand clutching her glass of liquor and the other on her hip was enough to grab my attention if I was an onlooker. Sinead sat in the chair that was to the left of me. There was a small table with the champagne on it separating us. She sat her drink on the table and turned towards me.

"What's your issue with me?"

The calmness in my voice in no way matched the way I was feeling on the inside. It was like I had just one good nerve left after that phone call, and I was pretty sure Sinead was going to trample it.

"What's my issue with you? Are you serious right now, Knight?" I thought that was a rhetorical question, so I remained quiet. She rolled her eyes and shook her head. "My issue with you is that you just cut me off with no kind of warning."

"No kind of warning?" I chuckled and sat up in my seat. "What kind of warning would you have liked for me to give you, Sinead? We weren't in a committed relationship. What would you have liked for me to have said or done?"

Sinead's attitude softened as did her stature in the seat. Her straight posture crumbled slightly as she lowered her head. Pulling it up, she looked into my eyes, and what I saw inside of them felt like a kick to my heart. It wasn't anger. It wasn't pain. It was love. She'd fallen for me. Hard.

"I don't know, Knight. More than a random call in the middle of the night to tell me we're done. I guess it's just... I had just spent time with you a week before that and we were fine. Then you call and call things off and..."

Cutting her off, I grabbed her hand from across the table and pulled it towards me.

"Sinead... what did I say when we first met? What did I say before I even accepted your number?" she tried to pull her hand away, but I held on. "What did I say, Sinead?"

"That you didn't want anything serious. That you wouldn't be consistent. That once this season was over I'd probably never hear from you again. That the most you could give me was random dates and sex when we were in the same city. But, Knight, even with you being so closed off you still treated me better than any other man has. I don't want to lose you."

She had me tempted to just stop messing with women completely. It didn't matter if I lied or told the truth, when it was time for things to be over they still gave me a hard time. During off seasons, that was my time to focus on myself. I fasted from women completely. Friendships weren't even allowed.

"I hear you, love, and I'm trying to be very sensitive to your feelings, but at this point I have nothing else to offer you. I'm sorry," I kissed her hand, put it on the table, and stood. "I'm gonna head out. Feel free to take this champagne. I'm sorry, Sinead."

Her head turned in the opposite direction and that made me feel worse, but I was tired of feeling bad. Tired of apologizing for leaving after I'd stressed from the beginning that I would. I was definitely cutting women off. Not just for the off season, but until I found one that understood me and was on the same level as me.

From this point forward my priority would be my family.

Charlie

I'd rehearsed my speech so many times I had it memorized, but I still couldn't work up the nerve to quit my job. For the past five years I've been the assistant manager at Bundled, a maternity store. Refusing multiple management positions forced me to face the truth – I hate my job. Okay, I don't really hate my job. I hate working for someone else for 12 hours a day just to make a multimillion dollar company even richer.

"Hello, Linda. Thank you so much for taking the time to speak with me. As you know I've worked for Bundled for the past five years, and although I love my job, I think it is time for me to go in another direction," I rushed out for what felt like the hundredth time as I paced around Linda's office.

Linda had been the general manager at my location for two years, but she'd been in her management field with the company for nine years.

"Maybe I shouldn't say another direction. But that's true," I mumbled before chewing on my cheek.

That other direction was turning my part time bedside service into a fulltime bedside service with a storefront and all. I'd been catering to the needs of pregnant women since my sister had her first child six years ago. That's actually what started my business. I did all of the ripping and running for her, and she suggested that I turn it into a business.

I'm not ashamed to admit it – fear is the sole reason I haven't gone fulltime with my business over the years. The security of working for a stable company made me comfortable, but I spend so much time here then so much time with my own business that I hardly have time for myself.

If I'm going to spend 12 hours a day working it just makes sense for me to spend 12 hours working for myself. Thankfully, I'd reached that point mentally... now I just needed to quit my job and make it happen.

"Hello, Linda. Thank you so much..." the door opened during my practice run, but instead of me turning around to face Linda, I shut my eyes, started over, and blurted my speech out. "Hello, Linda!" *why am I so loud?* "Thank you so much for taking the time to speak with me. As you know I've worked for..."

"Woah, woah. Wait. Not Linda. It's me."

My eyes opened as I turned to face Brea. She was a new hire that I'd taken under my wing three months ago.

"What are you doing here? Where's Linda?"

"She got caught up with a customer. She told me to come back here and let you know she was running behind but she'd be on her way soon," Brea closed the door behind her and leaned against it with a small smile. "You thinking about quitting?"

I nodded and leaned against Linda's desk. It had taken me two weeks to work up the nerve to ask to speak to her. Waiting for even two more seconds felt like the ultimate torture.

"Yep. It's been time."

"I'd hate to see you go seeing as you're the only other black person that works this shift with me, but I know how dedicated you are to your business and I really want to see it soar."

A small smile tilted the left side of my mouth, but it fell when the door opened again. Brea pulled herself off of it and winked at me as she exited. Not wanting to make my nervousness too apparent, I ran my hands down my pants before pulling my hands behind my back.

"Hey, lady. What's on your mind?" Linda made her way behind her desk and plopped down with a satisfied release of breath. "God, you have no idea how glad I am to sit down. Well, yes you do. You work harder than me around here. I honestly don't know what I'd do without you, Charlie. I'm trying to get these new hires up to speed and on the same level as you, but that seems like it's impossible. If I could have just three more of you I'd be satisfied. You can't ever leave me," she chuckled as she grabbed her bottle of Coke and took a swig. Motioning for me to sit down she ordered me to, "Sit down. Tell me what's on your mind."

With my bottom lip twisted to the side, I sat down and ran over my speech in my head.

"Hello, Linda," she looked at me with one raised eyebrow and a crooked smile. "Thank you so much for taking the…" I palmed my forehead and sighed. I've said this shit I don't know how many times. How could I be forgetting it right now? Just start over, Charlie. *Damn.* "Hello, Linda. Thank you so much for taking the time to speak with me. As you know…"

Knocks on the door interrupted my spill, and I cannot lie, I was kind of glad. I was like three words away from melting into a puddle of sad sweat. Just straight up pitiful, spineless, gullible sweat.

"Sorry guys, there's a lady out here that wants a cash refund for her purchase, but she doesn't have a receipt. I offered to give her store credit but she doesn't want it. Can one of you come talk to her?" Ava, another new hire asked.

"Sure. We'll be out in just a second. Charlie has…"

"No. It's. It can wait. I'll. Let me…" I stood and grabbed my phone off the edge of the desk. "I'll take care of the customer. It can wait."

"Are you sure?"

Closing the door behind me was my answer. I leaned my body against it softly for a few seconds before inhaling a deep breath, shaking my disappointment in myself off, and heading for the front of the store.

"Auntie Lie?" my youngest niece called.

I lifted her to my lap as I kept my attention on my Facebook feed.

"What's up, booger?"

"What's a set up?"

"What do you mean?"

"Mommy and daddy are in their room talking about a set up. Daddy is mad at mommy because he said she needs to stay out of your business, but mommy said it's her job as your sister to be in your business."

I sat my phone down and gave my full attention to Ariel.

"What did you just say?"

I know Veronica wasn't trying to set me up on another blind date. Ariel shrugged and grabbed the pendant on my necklace that she tried to talk me into letting her have every time she saw it. Little did she know... I'd purchased her her very on for Christmas.

"Mommy said you need to be set up. What's a set up? Why do you need to be set up?"

For once I was glad that Ariel was just as nosey as her meddling mother.

"I don't need to be set up, Ariel. Your mother is just..." with a groan I put Ariel on her feet and stood. "Just difficult for no reason."

With my phone in my hand, I placed a kiss on her forehead and headed for Veronica and Greg's bedroom. Sure enough, they were in the middle of a heated conversation that was immediately cut off at the sight of me.

"He – hey, Lie. How long have you been standing there?" Veronica asked with a fake smile.

"I'm going home."

"You're not staying for dinner?"

"No. I'm not in the mood for steaks and set ups."

"Set ups? Charlie…"

"No, V. I told you not to do this shit anymore. I told you no more blind dates. You promised!"

"I… it's not a blind date, Charlie!" Greg did one of those *I can't believe what I'm hearing* chuckles and walked away from her. When he made it to me he squeezed my shoulder before leaving. "I simply suggested that Chris…"

"Chris? The creepy guy that plays piano at church? Really, Veronica?"

"He's not creepy."

"He is creepy. He sweats all the time."

"It's hot up there when he's playing!"

"That is *not* a good excuse. Chris has sweat dripping down his bald head as soon as he gets to church, V. I cannot *believe* you tried to set me up with him!"

"But he's nice! You need a nice man…"

"No I don't. I don't even have time to date anyone. Why can't you and ma understand that? I'm not using that as an excuse. I honestly do not have the time to date, Veronica. When I have the time, trust me, I won't have any trouble meeting a man on my own. Step off."

Her eyes watered like the drama queen she is, and immediately I regretted being so harsh with her. It hardly ever happened. I was the nice sister. In fact, it only happened when she did stupid shit like this. I walked over to her and gave her the most forced hug I felt like I'd ever given in my life. I didn't want to comfort her for pissing me off. I just wanted to be pissed and go home!

"Don't cry, Veronica. It's not that serious. I'm sorry for snapping. You just get on my nerves sometimes when you do stuff like this. I keep telling you over and over and over and…"

"OK. OK. I get it. I won't try to hook you up again, but if you let 30 years of your life fly by because you're so focused on working that you miss out on what's most important don't blame me. And don't expect my kids to take care of you. You want someone to wipe your ass and keep you from getting bed sores… have your own kids."

"I do not plan on staying single for 30 years, Veronica. And in 30 years I won't even be old enough to need someone to take care of me. Do you hear yourself?"

"Auntie Ruth said the same thing and look at her."

She had a point. Our aunt was so focused on proving that she didn't need a man that she'd let her entire life float right by without having one. And by the time she realized she wanted one… it was too late. Well, it wasn't too late, but she was no longer concerned with dating at the age of 60, so she spent the rest of her days alone.

I released Veronica and put some space between us.

"I won't be like her."

"Just stay for dinner and talk…"

"No."

"Maybe you guys could just exchange…"

"Veronica…"

"Fine. I'm going to look really bad if you leave, Lie."

"That's not my concern. You should've thought about that before you invited him over."

I kissed her forehead just as I'd done Ariel before turning and leaving. Ignoring her protests, I pulled up my Chili's app and started a to go order. Forget what she was talking about. I was not about to spend one of the few free nights I had having an awkward dinner with her, Greg, and Chris. An appetizer combo and a few movies would do me just right.

KNIGHT

This was not how I planned on spending my first day of the off season. First of all, I didn't plan on being home at all. I planned on being in Miami somewhere on the beach with a few drinks. Not sitting outside of Harlem's best friend's house waiting for her to come out. Last night I could barely sleep. My baby sister was pregnant. She was only 16 and she was pregnant.

That had been eating at me all night.

I had no clue who the father was. What their relationship status was. If he planned on sticking around. If his parents knew. None of that. But it was my goal to have all of my questions answered by the end of the day.

The creaking of the door opening grabbed my attention. I put my phone down and looked towards the door. Princess had one bag and Harlem had the other as they made their way to my car. Getting out, I said a silent prayer that I wouldn't be too hard on her. Harlem was tough, but I was the only person she softened for. I was the only person whose opinion seemed to matter to her.

We had that alike. Tough and hard hearted for everyone but those we kept close. For them we were soft and easily wrecked. That's why she tried to stay clear of Carmen. She already had enough to deal with dealing with pops. Dealing with judgment from an older sister who tried way too hard to be her mother was a stress Harlem didn't want or need.

Nodding at Princess, I grabbed the bags from both girls and my eyes immediately lowered to Harlem's stomach.

"Hey, Knight," Princess spoke. "Thanks again for those tickets for my dad's birthday."

I nodded but kept my eyes on Harlem's stomach. It stuck out a little but not much. Because of the tight shirt she had on it looked like she'd stuffed herself with food and had a little gut. Shopping for clothes that fit was now at the top of the list of things to do today.

"No problem. Are your parents' home? I want to thank them for letting her stay."

"They haven't made it in from work yet."

"Cool. I'll stop by a little later then."

Princess nodded and pulled Harlem in for a hug. She whispered something that I couldn't hear in Harlem's ear that caused her to smile and nod, then she let her go and walked back to her house.

Harlem and I stood there – just staring at each other. Well, she was staring at me. I was staring at her stomach. Harlem crossed her arms over her chest and shifted her weight to her left side.

"Are you going to just stand there staring at me all day, Knight?"

"I just can't believe you've got a baby in there."

My eyes met hers finally and she smiled. I smiled. This was still my baby sister. She was still my pride and joy.

"Believe it. It's real."

"Can I... touch it?"

Harlem chuckled and rolled her eyes as she nodded. I put her bags in the backseat and walked over to her. Even though I asked, I had a hard time actually touching her stomach. Her small hand grabbed mine and she placed it on her stomach. It wasn't as hard as I thought it would be, but it definitely felt like something was in there.

"What happened, Harlem? I mean I know what happened but..."

With a shake of my head I pulled my hand away and opened the passenger door for her. She walked over to it slowly and looked up at me instead of getting right in.

"I know you're probably disappointed in me, boo, but I really didn't plan for this to happen. I'm sorry."

Unsure of what to say, I nodded and motioned for her to get in the car. We had nothing but time to talk. There was no point in rushing it now.

I thought I'd take her to a regular store and she could buy some stuff that was a few sizes bigger than her size, but Harlem told me that she wanted to go to an actual maternity store. That was cool. I wanted her to have all that wanted and needed. She chose a store called Bundled that I'd never even heard of before. We pulled up, and I was bound and determined to sit in the car and wait, but she suckered me into coming in anyway.

Apparently I wasn't the only man in that position. There were three others that were sitting on a bench in front of the window. I wasted no time sitting next to them and joining them. Thankful that I had my earbuds with me, I grabbed them out of my pocket, connected them to my phone, and got some music going. I was pretty sure this was going to take a while, so I leaned my head against the window and prepared to get me a little nap in.

It felt like just as soon as my body started relaxing I was being nudged in the shoulder. My eyes opened slowly to the sight of Harlem pointing towards the section where they had car seats and shit, but I couldn't focus on those. My focus was on the beautiful woman standing in front of the car seats.

She had big, wild tight curls in her hair. Very big and wild and tight curls. They were long and full and just... everywhere. Smooth brown skin covered her toned frame. From a distance it looked to be blemish free, but I couldn't be sure. Her skin had a reddish tint, but it was the same brown as acorns.

I wanted to taste it.

At first glance, I wasn't expecting her to actually be working here because of what she had on. She was dressed in a white button down shirt dress. It stopped mid-thigh, and she had on a pair of white sandals with it. The dress was the right length to give me the perfect view of her slim thick thighs.

She laughed and pulled my attention back to her face. The sound of her laugh was the most beautiful laugh I've ever heard in my life. It sounded so… full. So full of life. And her smile… she had the biggest, brightest smile I'd ever seen. It took over her whole face. As beautiful as her dark tight eyes were, I think I liked them better squinted and practically closed as she laughed.

She took the papers from the girl that had said whatever it was that made her laugh, then returned her attention to the car seats. Now I was only blessed with a side view of her, but I'd take that too. Baby was beautiful on all sides.

"Knight! I said come look at the car seats with me," Harlem said for what I gathered to be the second time before walking away and returning to the car seats.

I scratched my chin as I looked the woman over once more. She was definitely my type. Beautiful real hair. Beautiful brown skin. Beautiful shape. Beautiful dark eyes. Beautiful smile and perfect white teeth. Just beautiful.

Remembering my fast, I stood and unwillingly made my way over to the car seats, Harlem, and the beauty. My nose was assaulted by a perfume that it didn't agree with, and I sneezed… which apparently caught the beauty off guard because she jumped in the most adorable way and dropped all of her papers.

"Dang, Knight! I told you about sneezing in public. Loud ass sneeze," Harlem scolded as she tried to bend and help the beauty pick up her papers, but she stopped her.

"No. No. I got it, sweetheart," sweetheart? "But thanks." I call her sweetheart.

Shaking whatever I was feeling off, I squatted to help the beauty pick up the papers. Her hands worked quickly to gather the papers, but when she looked into my eyes they stopped moving. And so did mine. Her smile fell. So did mine.

"Apologize, boo."

I heard Harlem, but I wasn't trying to see her. I didn't want anything or anyone taking away from my view of this beauty.

"I apologize," I offered.

The beauty smiled that beautiful smile before lowering her eyes to the ground.

"It's OK. Your sneeze just scared a little life out of me."

I chuckled as I grabbed the rest of the papers and handed them to her. We stood at the same time but she put some space between us.

"My bad. I know it can be loud, so I try to hold it in as much as I can."

"You don't have to apologize for that. It's natural."

With a nod, I put my hands in my pockets to avoid touching her hair. I knew how naturals were about their hair. That was definitely not a battle I wanted to endure again. Not without her permission at least.

"OK, Knight, I can't choose between these two," Harlem pulled me by the arm towards her. "Red or black?"

"I thought you were picking out clothes today?"

"I was, but we might as well get as much as we can today; unless you want to make another trip so you can flirt with that lady some more."

The beauty was standing off to the side, but I saw her eyes widen out of the corner of my eye before her shoulders tensed and she busied herself further away from us.

"Really, Harlem? Why would you say that?"

"It's the truth."

"I was *not* flirting with her."

"Whatever. Help me pick out a seat."

"I ain't helping you pick out shit."

"Knight! Come on now! Don't start being mean! If you don't help me do this kind of stuff who will?"

"Where's the dude that's responsible for this?"

"Responsible for this? This? Did you call my baby a *this*?"

Now she was about to start acting crazy.

"Um…" the beauty walked back over to us timidly. "I didn't mean to eavesdrop, but… if your boyfriend…"

"Boyfriend? This meanie is my big brother," Harlem quickly corrected.

The beauty bit down on her top lip as long as she could before a smile appeared. She nodded and inhaled deeply.

"Oh. OK. If your brother doesn't want to help with this kind of stuff, allow me. I have a bedside service business. I make baskets for expecting mothers. I offer pre and post delivery services such as shopping, baby registry and birth announcements, nursey design, diaper delivery, laundry service, hospital prep, baby shower planning and throwing, pampering, and…" she gestured towards the car seats, "I put together packages filled with things you'll need from Bundled including car seats," the beauty pulled one of the papers she'd dropped out of the stack and handed it to Harlem. "Here's a list of everything in the store. If you want, you can walk around the store and make a list of everything you want and need. Then I'll get it all together for you and deliver it."

Harlem grabbed my forearm, "Knight," she shook it, "Can we have her?"

The beauty blushed and lowered her head.

"Harlem, go somewhere. Let me talk to her for a second."

"Fine."

Harlem turned her attention to the clothes, what she should've been looking at in the first place, and allowed me to have the beauty to myself.

"Sorry about my sister. I have no excuse to offer besides she's just crazy."

The beauty smiled, and I couldn't help but wonder how it would feel to see that every day for the rest of my life. Blessing.

"She's cute. She reminds me of my older sister when we were younger."

Her hand went to the collar of her dress and she squeezed it as if being around me made her uncomfortable.

"So… bedside service?"

"Right. Right. I also make doctor's appointments when you or the father can't go with her. I'm basically there every step of the way for whatever you guys need. Even random calls at midnight because she's craving dill pickle chips and ice cream."

"How does this work? And how much does it cost?"

"Well, my website is on the bottom of the paper I gave your sister. All of my packages are listed there. I like to meet with my clients and get a feel for what they will need before I suggest a package, but they range from five hundred to five thousand depending on how present you want me to be."

"Cool. I'm sure we'll just end up taking the biggest one. Your contact information on that paper as well?"

"Yep."

"You know what? Can we just set up a time to meet now? I want to help her all that I can, but I can already tell we're not going to get along much and I'm going to need all the help I can get."

The beauty smiled again.

That smile was going to get her pretty ass in trouble.

"That's perfectly fine. I'm here a lot, but if you can give me a second to grab my planner I'll let you know my availability."

"Sounds good."

She took a few steps back before walking off to the side and behind me. Not caring if it was obvious or not, I turned around to get a view of her ass. Nice little small yet round ass. It was small enough to not be too much, but enough for me to grab a handful of. Her hips were curvy, and her waist was small, but it was natural looking. Not like she spent every day at the gym in one of those waist shapers.

While I waited for her to return I looked around the store for Harlem who was now looking at baby bags.

"OK, so... it looks like I'm available... in two days. Saturday. Will that work?"

I turned at the sound of the beauty's voice. She had her head in her planner, so she didn't see me checking her out. Even if she did I really didn't care. I just... couldn't stop looking at her.

"Yea, that'll work. What time?"

She met my eyes again and smiled.

"Noon?"

"Cool. I'll have Harlem text you my address."

"OK, well, it was nice meeting you..."

I extended my hand for hers. She looked down at it and back at me before putting her hand inside of mine.

"Knight Carver."

Her head tilted to the side as I pulled her a little closer to me.

"Knight Carver? The sports announcer for the Grizzlies? I thought your face was a little familiar."

"You into basketball?"

"Just the Grizzlies. I love going to their games."

I nodded. That gave her even more points in my book. But I was fasting. With that recollection I released her hand.

"That's what's up. Yea, that's me. And you are?"

"Charlie White."

"Nice to meet you, Charlie."

The beauty... Charlie... wrapped her arm around her stomach and grabbed her elbow.

"Nice to meet you too. And... Harlem?"

I nodded and looked at Harlem briefly.

"Saturday at noon?"

"Saturday at noon."

"OK."

"OK."

This was the end of the conversation I'm sure, but my feet wouldn't move. Neither could my eyes.

"Charlie, can you come show me how to apply the coupon again?" somebody behind the register asked, but I didn't see.

All I saw was the beauty.

All I saw was Charlie.

And even though I didn't know anything about her... there was something about her aura that told me she needed to be seen.

901-612-9909: Hey, Charlie! This is Harlem (the girl from Bundled with the brother whose sneeze scared you) I can't wait to meet with you today! Here's our address – 5427 Valley Springs Dr. Call if you need help finding the place – Harlem

I stared at Harlem's text as I waited for Doctor Berry to join me in his office. This would be the first client meeting that I've been this excited about in a while! My excitement didn't stem from the money I could potentially make, although that played a part in it, I was more excited about being around Knight.

Yes, I had absolutely no plans of dating and getting into a relationship right now, but there was something about him that I just… really, *really* liked. It went beyond his looks and I couldn't quite put my finger on what it was. Don't get me wrong, though, Knight Carver was very nice on the eyes.

He had the sexiest chestnut skin. You know, that sexy shade of brown that meant he had no trouble snatching panties. It was the kind of brown that wrapped around men of a certain kind of breed. The kind of brown that embraced his manhood. His blackness. His power. His sexy. His… *him*. The kind of brown that just looked damn good. And smooth. And edible. And right.

Knight had that boy next door handsome. He was the kind of handsome that you might miss if you walked past him on the street, but once you set eyes on him… you'd never forget him. His hair was cut into a low tapered fade. Straight brows and dark ebony eyes gave him a no nonsense kind of look. He had the kind of eyes that felt like they were questioning you. Looking into you and questioning the depths of you; and there was nothing you could do but allow them to.

Knight's beard was more scruff than anything. It wasn't like he was trying to grow it out to fit a trend. It was like... that had been his style for years. Like he just didn't give a damn. Like he was rough and bad yet clean and good. I don't know. The small amount of hair just fit him perfectly.

I think I liked his lips the most. His classic, full lips. The top one was the color of his skin while the bottom one was deep pink. Pink! And it was just a tad bigger than the top one. Those lips were the first thing I noticed on his face, and as soon as I saw them I couldn't help but wonder how they would feel.

How they would taste.

Now that I think about it, I noticed *way* too much about him in that short amount of time. Memorized too much about him in that short amount of time. If I was going to be working with his sister, and it seemed like the job was pretty much guaranteed at this point, I needed to steer clear of this. These... feelings. This desire. This lust. I never lust. *Ever*.

"So sorry to keep you waiting, Charlie," Doctor Berry spoke as he walked into his office and closed the door behind him. "How've you been?"

"Good, Dr. Berry. You?"

"Good," he sat across from me behind his desk and smiled as he let out a tight exhale. "How's that heart treating you?"

As usual, my response to anyone asking about my heart was to rub it absently. Well, I guess it wasn't really *my* heart. It wasn't the one I was born with. I had open heart surgery when I was 19, and now... I had the heart of Angela Carver.

"Great. Just great."

"Amazing. You know, out of 10 years, your testimony is the one I love telling the most. You were definitely saved by God that night, Charlie. He saved you. Your heart stopped just at the same time Angela's husband decided to take her off of life support. And the fact that she'd requested that her heart be donated to you..."

My eyes watered as I lowered my head. No matter the amount of time, the topic of Angela always got to me. She was literally like my angel here on earth. She'd been in the hospital a little less than me, but on one of our emergency room visits together, I was placed in a separate room in ICU. As I was getting settled in with IV's being put on me and all of that, she was getting ready to head home.

I didn't know anything about Angela then, not even her name. She walked past my little area and because the curtain was slightly open, she was able to look in at me. I guess I looked young and out of place to her because her face scrunched up as she turned to get a better look at me.

Doctor Berry came over, and they talked amongst themselves. He told her that I was there with heart complications, and that the only hope I really had at that point was to have a heart transplant. To my surprise, no, to my grace, she told Doctor Berry that she was a registered donor, and that when the time came, she wanted to donate her heart to me.

I'd never gotten to talk to her. I didn't even know until after the surgery had been performed and my parents told me. All I had was her act of kindness and what Doctor Berry said she said when she made the offer.

He asked her why she wanted to do such a thing for a total and complete stranger, and she said that I was less of a stranger than any of us thought. That she wanted her heart to continue to beat even after she was gone. And I was too young to die if there was something she could do about it. The part about me being less of a stranger still didn't make any sense to me, but I'd learned long ago to not question it and just thank God and Angela Carver.

"I'm sorry, Charlie, I don't want to make you cry. That just… blows my mind every time I see you. But anyway, our annual charity week is coming up. I can imagine the load you have on your shoulders with working and running a business, but I was wondering if you could volunteer this year? We could really use a fresh mind with new creativity. We've been doing kind of the same thing over the years because of the volunteer community we have, and because of that, we've been pulling in the same amount of money. This year I want to try something different in hopes of pulling in new sponsors and donations."

There was no way I could turn Doctor Berry down. Not after how good he'd been to my family and I over the years. But he was right… I had a lot on my plate. I guess it was a matter of priority at this point. I owed a lot to him, his staff, and this hospital. If they needed my help putting their event together, that's what they'd have.

It was their charity events over the years that helped to pay for my medicine, treatments, copays, and bills when my parents' insurance said they'd reached their cap. Yea, they would definitely have my help.

Five minutes into my drive I received a call from one of my most difficult clients. Bianca. Her father spoiled her before she left home, and her husband picked up, so she had this spirit of entitlement that rubbed me the wrong way every time I was around her. Had I known what I was signing up for I wouldn't have taken her on as a client, but all of my initial meetings were done with her husband. I didn't meet Bianca until my first day working with them.

I've been dreading signing that contract ever since.

I started to not answer. I started to just not answer, but the longer I looked at her name on my phone the more I remembered that a part of our agreement was that I be available 24/7. The only time I could put one client off was if I was with another. With the fakest cheerful voice I could muster, I answered Bianca's call.

"Hey, Bianca."

"Charlie! Where are you? I need you."

"I'm on the way to meet with a potential client, B. What's wrong, honey?"

"I can't tie my shoes."

My countenance fell at her admission. Was she really calling me because she couldn't tie her shoes? Did she really want me to stop what I was doing to come and tie her shoes? No. That... she... no.

"What did you just say?"

"I said I can't tie my shoes, Charlie. I'm supposed to go for a walk to try and get this baby out of me, but I can't tie my shoes."

If she didn't sound so distraught I would've laughed, but this was her first baby and it had proven to be an adjustment for her to share her body with someone else.

"OK, Bianca, why don't you take the shoes off, tie them, then put them on?"

Her voice grew cold and low as she said, "You think I didn't think about that, Charlie? I can't get the shoes off the floor. Kevin put them on me before he left for work and I... I just need you to come and tie them for me."

Never mind the fact that she could've gotten one of her neighbors to do it. Never mind the fact that she could've used a broom or pair of tongs to pick up the shoes. This was typical spoiled Bianca.

"Fine, Bianca. Give me about 15 minutes."

"15 minutes? You can't get here any faster than that?"

"Girl, you better..."

"OK. OK. Thanks, Charlie. You're the best."

With a nod I disconnected the call and pulled up Harlem's text. I called the number to let her know I'd be a few minutes late.

"Yea?" Knight answered and completely caught me off guard. So off guard I had to pull the phone from my ear to make sure I'd dialed the right number. "Hello?"

"Oh. Yea. Sorry. Um, I was looking for Harlem. She texted me from this number."

"Charlie?"

Why was I biting my cheek to avoid smiling at hearing him say my name?

"Yea. I was just calling to let her, well you now, know that I'm going to be a few minutes late. One of my clients just called and asked me to come and tie her shoes so…"

"Yo…" I could hear the chuckle in his voice as he cut what I assumed to be the radio in his car down. "Are you serious? People actually call you for that kind of stuff?"

"You'd be surprised."

"That's fine. I'm on my way home now so I'll tell Harlem when I get there. I don't know why she texted you from my phone instead of hers. I guess because I'll be the one handling the business, but I'll let her know you're going to be a few minutes late."

"Great, thanks."

I was about to disconnect the call, ready to get his voice out of my ear and head, but he called my name and regained my attention.

"Charlie?"

"Yea?"

"Um, I'm going to stop and grab something to eat. Maybe some wings. You… want something?"

Not able to answer him right away, I allowed my smile to form as I shook my head.

"That's very sweet of you, but I'm still full from breakfast. Thank you, though, Knight."

"Cool. Well, I guess I'll see you in a few."

"K."

I ended the call and any irritation I felt that was caused by Bianca's random call had dissolved.

KNIGHT

Before Charlie came over I wanted to talk to pops about how involved he was going to be, and talk to Harlem about the baby's daddy. As of now he was just a sperm donor to me, but she seemed to be kind of sensitive right now so I was trying to respect her feelings. We didn't talk much the first day she was at my spot, but we had to have that talk when I got home.

I needed to know how much was going to be required of me. As I sat in front of the home I grew up in so many different thoughts and feelings rushed through me. When my mom died I was on the road. It was my first year starting for the Grizzlies. I wasn't able to come home much because of that, and after she died I really kept my distance.

The relationship that my pops and I had was one of understanding and respect. He understood that I didn't respect some of the ways he handled things, and I understood the fact that he didn't give a damn what I thought and how I felt.

As long as we didn't stay around each other for too long we were good, which is why I wanted to keep this visit as quick as I possibly could. The goal was to get in, ask about Harlem, and get the hell out.

I made my way up to the front door, and instead of using my key to let myself in I knocked on the door. About a minute passed before he was letting me in. We shook hands and I led the way to the living room. We shook hands. I haven't seen my father in six months and we greet each other by shaking hands.

Wasting no time, as soon as we sat down I jumped right in.

"So, I just wanna know what you planning on doing for Harlem and the baby."

He looked at me like I'd asked him to name all 50 states in alphabetical order. With a low chuckle, he shook his head and leaned back in his seat.

"I'm not doing anything for her and the baby. I made it very clear to her when she left what her options were. If she wanted to be grown she was going to do it on her own and get out of my house. If she wanted to continue to live here and let me raise her and provide for her she was going to have to get rid of it. I ain't raising no more kids. None."

"You told her to get an abortion?"

He shrugged and exhaled loudly as he swallowed.

"I'm not raising no more kids."

"Apparently you're not even raising her so why would I expect you to help her?"

"Watch it, Knight."

I stood. Disappointed. But that shouldn't surprise me. He'd been disappointing me ever since my mama died.

"It's cool. I'll take care of her and the baby like mama would've wanted me to. I can't believe you."

"Your mama would've wanted her to finish school and go to college before letting some boy knock her up."

"We're past that now. Obviously that's not going to happen. Now we have to come up with a plan of action for the position she's in now. She's your daughter, not mine. She's 16 years old. And you're sitting here telling me that you're not going to do anything to help her?"

He crossed his arms over his chest and stared at me.

"Fuck it. I don't even know why I wasted my time even coming over here."

"I don't either. You don't come around for nothing else."

"Why should I? Every time I do it's some shit. I'm tired of fighting with you all the time."

"There wouldn't be a fight if you bowed down and showed me some respect."

"Bowed down?" my voice was raising right along with my anger, and he was just sitting there with the most nonchalant look on his face. "Show you some respect? I respect the God in you as a human being, but you've done nothing extra to gain more of my respect. All of the respect I had for you died right along with my mother."

"Will you let that go? What did you want me to do, son?"

"I wanted you to fight! I wanted you to fight for us! For her!"

"She was brain dead! The fuck did you want me to do? She was a vegetable! There was nothing I could do!"

"But you didn't even try," my voice softened as my eyes watered.

No matter how much time passed, I could never get over the day she died. How he was so quick to pull the plug on her. That did something to me. Made me feel like he didn't really love her. Didn't really love us. In my mind I knew that wasn't true... but in my heart it was.

"Knight, there was nothing I could do. She was tired of fighting, and honestly so was I."

"Oh. So that's what this is about? You. You were tired of taking care of her so you just let her die?"

"That's not what I'm saying and you know it. I was the one that was here all day every day with her while she was suffering and you were out being the big NBA superstar. The only thing she asked of you was that you finish your degree before you started in the NBA and you didn't even give her that!"

"You don't think I know that?! You think that doesn't eat at me every day of my fucking life? Why do you think I quit the league right after she died? I don't need you throwing that shit up in my face every time I come around. That's why I don't come around. I feel guilty enough about not being here for her before she died. I don't need you throwing it in my face. I refuse to not be here for Harlem. So you don't have to worry about doing shit for her and the baby. I'll take care of it all."

"Knight..."

I couldn't get out of there fast enough.

"Sweetheart!" I yelled as soon as I stepped foot in my home.

"What, boo?" was her response from her room upstairs.

"Get down here. I need to talk to you before Charlie gets here."

Heading into the kitchen with our food, I scratched her father's name off my mental list of people she'd have to count on. Now I needed to see if she could depend on her sperm donor. If not, it would be up to me and Carmen. Mostly me since Carmen wasn't even in town. She didn't even come home yesterday like she said she was, but she was going to fly in tonight. And Charlie. Somehow, her being in the equation made it seem like we had more than enough help.

It was the middle of the day, and after my conversation with Carmen and Harlem's father, because I didn't even consider him mine anymore, I felt like I needed a shot of something. Harlem's feet shuffling down the stairs stopped me. I walked into the living room and found her laying on the couch in her pajamas.

"Why did you text Charlie from my phone? And why aren't you dressed? She'll be here soon."

"Did you bring food, boo? I smell it," I didn't answer her as I sat on the opposite side of the couch. "I texted Charlie from your phone because I figured you'll be the one she's going to be talking to while we figure this out, so it makes more sense for her to have your number instead of mine. It's only going to take me three seconds to throw on a pair of sweats."

"Seasoned wings on the table in the..." I couldn't even get it out good before she was jumping up and heading to the kitchen. "Kitchen. Eat in here. We need to talk."

As I waited for her to return I thought over Charlie's unexpected call. She had no idea how hearing from her completely lightened my mood. I was pissed as hell when I left Carmen and Harlem's father's house, but hearing her voice for whatever reason seemed to have soothed me. We weren't even on the phone for three minutes and in less than three minutes she'd completely turned my mood around, but when I pulled into my driveway and prepared to talk to Harlem my attitude slowly returned.

"OK," Harlem tossed a fry into her mouth as she returned to the living room and sat down. "Let me have it. You haven't yelled at me yet. Go on and get it over with."

"I'm not going to yell at you; I just have some questions I need you to answer," Harlem put the wings in the middle of us and I grabbed one and ate it before I asked my first question. "Your sperm donor..."

"Can you not call him that, Knight?"

"At this point that's all he is. I haven't heard you talk to him not once over these past two days. He's not a father in my eyes. He's a sperm donor. If he steps up that will change, but as of now... he's a sperm donor. Who is he, how old is he, and how did you meet him?"

"His name is Tage..."

"Tage? The fuck kind of name is Tage?"

"Knight!"

"All right, continue."

I grabbed a wing and started eating it to avoid interrupting her again.

"His name is Tage. He's 17. He's a junior. We go to school together. I met him last year."

"Are you in a relationship with him or were you just having sex with him?"

There was no doubt about it – this was a very uncomfortable conversation for the both of us, but it was one that we had to have. She sighed and put her half eaten wing back in the foil pan.

"We are in a relationship. We were in a relationship. When I told him that I was pregnant he fell back. So to answer your future questions no I don't expect him to be involved. No I don't expect him to support his child. No I don't expect him to even tell his parents that he has a baby on the way. He says he's going to.

He says he's going to come with me to the doctor and stuff but... I just don't believe him. You always say let actions speak and I ain't hearing nothing from him right now. He has been calling and texting, but that just doesn't mean anything to me right now."

She picked her wing back up and finished it off as I smiled. As messed up as this situation was, I was proud that she wasn't out here living young and naïve completely. At least she listened to *some* of the stuff I told her.

"We'll see what he does. I'm going to warn you, though, if he's going to be involved he will have to be all in. I'm not playing that inconsistent half in half out bullshit. Page is..."

"Tage, Knight. Tage."

"He is going to have to tell his parents and step up to the plate if he wants to be in the baby's life. None of that hiding y'all from his family and coming around when he wants to randomly pop up shit. He'll have to get a job and help you in some way, Harlem, just on the strength of him getting you pregnant. You won't need the money, and I'd suggest you put it in a savings account for the baby's college fund or something, but he needs to invest something besides his seed in you."

If there was one thing she'd never have to worry about it was money. My first year of college I was drafted and joined the Memphis Grizzles. I played in the NBA for four years before I retired, and I didn't touch any of the money I made playing ball until I retired. For those four years I lived solely off advertisement deals.

I had enough money saved to never have to work again a day in my life. Announcing for the Grizzlies was my way of still being connected to the game in some way. Basketball was my passion and probably would always be, and in the small amount of time that I played professionally, it set me up for life.

"That's fair. Knight, I'm sorry. I know you had these big dreams for me…"

"It doesn't matter what dreams I had for you. I want you to live for you and your baby. We're good. Things happen. I'm not going to lie and say I wasn't hurt when you told me, but I'm not going to punish you for this, Harlem. I feel like you got enough of that from your father. And that's going to happen from everybody else in the family. They're going to give you hell. They will love your child and accept him or her wholeheartedly, but they're going to give you hell. You don't need that from me."

Harlem smiled as she stood and sat next to me. Her arms wrapped around my neck and she kissed my cheek.

"That's why you're my fave. I love you, Knight."

"I love you too. Now finish feeding my niece."

"Nephew."

"How you know?"

"I don't. I just don't want a girl."

"Why not?"

"Too high maintenance."

"Whatever. When is your next appointment?"

"Next Friday. We can find out then what I'm having."

I nodded and stood to go into the kitchen. The wings were good, but I needed something to wash them down with. After grabbing a bottle of water out of the refrigerator I headed over to the table to get my phone. The blinds on the window were open, and the sight of a yellow beetle pulling into my driveway made me smile. That car fit Charlie perfectly. Fit her smile perfectly.

I felt like I should've turned away, or at least headed to the front door to let her in, but I found myself standing there watching her. Watching her cut her car off. Close her eyes and take a few deep breaths. Lean over and grab her purse and another bag out of the passenger seat. Open the door, lock her car, and make her way to the front door.

In another one of those button down shirt dresses. This one was red. I loved the way the white complemented her skin, but the red one gave her a sexy edge that wasn't there the first day I met her.

Since she was no longer in my sight I was able to snap out of it and walk away. The doorbell rang, and Harlem made no attempt to answer it as she took the pan of wings upstairs with her. I was happy to be seeing her again. Maybe a little too eager to see her. Toning that feeling down, I reminded myself of my fast as I went to the door to let her in. Besides, there was nothing about Charlie that said friend with benefits.

I opened the door and was met by that beautiful smile.

"Hi," she spoke soft yet bubbly.

She had that happy hippie kind of vibe that made me chuckle.

"What's up? Come in."

Charlie stepped inside and waited for me to close the door and lead her into the living room.

"Wow. You have a beautiful home, Knight."

"Thanks. Have a seat."

I would've offered her a tour of the place, but I figured she'd get that if we decided to do business together.

"Where's Harlem?"

"Present," we both looked at Harlem as she came down the stairs. "Hey, Charlie."

"Hey, sweetheart. How you feeling?"

"Good. A little hungry, but I'll finish eating after you leave."

"That's not necessary. You can eat now. Feed that baby."

Harlem smiled and nodded as she returned to her room to grab the wings. Charlie returned her attention to me.

"Did you guys have a chance to look at my website?"

I cleared my throat and readjusted myself in my seat. The day we met, I wasn't as aware of her scent as I was right now. Maybe it had worn off over the course of the day, but right now... I could smell her, and the combination of a woman that looked good and smelled good had always been my weakness.

It wasn't just the fact that she had on a perfume that smelled good or nothing simple like that. It smelled like it was made for her. It mixed with her natural scent perfectly. And even though I knew she was wearing some type of perfume, it was so natural that it smelled like it could literally come straight from her pores. Intoxicating. Commanding.

"You smell *very* good," I heard myself say, but I was hoping and praying I'd said it under my breath.

When she blushed and lowered her head I knew I'd said it out loud.

"Thank you. So do you."

Now that pulled a laugh out of me because I knew I smelled straight up like the Mary Jane filled blunt I smoked on my way home. That was my only vice I guess. Maybe not the only one, but the only one that I had absolutely no plans of ever changing.

"Thank you. I do smoke daily, but not in the house so you don't have to worry about this being a bad environment for Harlem and the baby."

"That thought never crossed my mind."

That statement. That statement created a silent thickness between us that wasn't broken until Harlem came back downstairs. Well, she made it down to the bottom step, looked between us, then started going back up the steps backwards.

"Sorry," she mouthed to me with a smile.

"Girl, get your silly ass over here," I said with my own smile – thankful for the pull away from Charlie's web.

Charlie fluffed her hair and inhaled deeply as Harlem sat next to her. Surprisingly close. Harlem was mean. Period. She had to trust you to be nice to you. I couldn't decipher if she was being nice to Charlie because she wanted Charlie's help, or if she sensed that Charlie was good people.

Charlie's hand went to Harlem's thigh in what looked like a natural response to Harlem being so close to her.

"How far along are you?"

"I'll be four months next week."

"Will you know what you're having next week? Or are you going to wait until he or she arrives?"

"I'm going to find out. I don't think I'd be able to wait any longer than I absolutely have to. Are you hungry?"

What? Harlem was offering someone her food? She never did that. The only reason I was able to eat the wings was because we'd had the same fight over the years. Now she didn't even fight me on it. She just accepted the fact that I was going to take whatever I wanted. From whoever I wanted.

"I'm good, sweetheart."

Charlie crossed her legs and the act pulled her dress up slightly. My eyes lowered and took in those smooth brown thighs. The desire to have them squeezing my neck as I devoured her shot through me so deeply my dick hardened. She sat back in her seat and put her arm behind Harlem. Just getting completely comfortable. And that was the sexiest shit I'd ever seen in my life. She looked like she belonged here. Maybe she did.

"So tell me what you need from me, Harlem."

Harlem smiled as she wiped her mouth and shrugged.

"I don't know. I guess I need you to like… help me with everything. My mom passed and my sister lives in another state, so it's really just me and Knight, and as you saw in the store we don't always get along."

Charlie's face softened when Harlem mentioned mama being gone, but she smiled when Harlem mentioned the other day. She shot me a quick look before returning her attention to Harlem.

"I'm so sorry to hear about your mom. I can't imagine how hard that is on you to be so young. You don't have to worry; I'll be with you every step of the way. Shopping, decorating, advice, appointments… whatever you need I got you."

Harlem nodded and returned to her wings as if that was all she needed to hear to be satisfied.

"So five thousand?" I asked pulling Charlie's eyes to mine.

She looked as if she wanted to say no, but nodded.

"Is that OK?"

"Perfectly fine. When can you start?"

"I usually don't start until my clients are five months. It gives them time to adjust before I barge in. And it allows them to try and handle everything on their own for a little while before I help. Kind of makes them…"

"Put some respeck on yo name," Harlem muttered with a mouth full of food.

Charlie giggled with a nod.

"Exactly."

"That's cool. Do you have the contract or…"

"I'll work it up when I get home and send it to you. I'll need your email address. After you sign you'll be directed to a link to pay at least half of my total as your deposit."

I nodded, but planned on paying the whole thing in full.

"Cool. Now that I have your number I'll lock it in and text you my email address."

"That'll work. Do you guys have any questions?"

"Nope. Your website was very well laid out. Anything I had to ask was answered on it."

"Good. Well, if you do have any questions feel free to call me. The contract will include the dates I'll be around to help, my availability, and what's included in your contract. If you have any questions as you go over it do not hesitate to reach out to me," Charlie pulled a couple of papers and brochures out of her bag. "These are for you guys to look over between now and when I start."

She stood to leave, and I found myself wanting her to stay.

"I'm gonna get out of you guys' way. I'm sure you have something planned to do on this beautiful Saturday. Even if it's just to chill."

She squeezed Harlem's shoulder softly, and Harlem blew her an air kiss.

"Actually, I planned on going out with my best friend, but I'm sure Knight doesn't have…"

"Harlem," I warned. I didn't know what the hell had gotten into her. Usually she hated me interacting with a woman around her. She was practically throwing me at Charlie today. "I'll walk you out, Charlie," I continued.

"Cool. See you, Harlem."

"Bye!"

I looked back at Harlem as Charlie and I walked to the front door. She stuck her tongue out at me, then hopped on the other side of the couch when I grabbed a pillow and threw it at her. Charlie was close as I opened the door, and the height difference was apparent. I looked down at her and she looked up at me with a soft smile.

I've never known anyone in my life to smile as much as she does. As crazy as my life has been, it's honestly refreshing, but I didn't need refreshing. Not while I was trying to stay committed to my fast. I didn't need that beautiful, bright smile shining into my soul like a light in darkness.

"Harlem is special," she almost whispered. "There's something within her that's going to change the world, Knight. I can't tell you what it is and how I know, but I feel it. Protect her purpose. Don't let this pregnancy ruin her."

Before I could stop myself I took her left hand into mine. She looked down at it intently. Like she was trying to figure something out. Charlie lifted our hands and got a closer look at mine.

"Your hands..." she shook her head and chewed on the inside of her cheek as her eyebrows wrinkled. "You have the most perfect hands. They're big like they could protect, but smooth like they could cherish."

Her right hand went on top of my hand as she used the left one to keep it secured. As she studied my hand I studied her. Feeling yet another piece of my strength turn flaccid.

"Is that a beauty mark?" her pointing finger ran across the mole as I called it on my middle finger. She looked up at me and her eyes grew wide as she pulled her hands away and put some space between us. "I'm so sorry. That was extremely weird of me and unprofessional."

She opened the door and stepped out.

"Charlie..."

"I'll send you the contract before five this evening. Enjoy the rest of your day."

"Char–"

Her back turned to me as she damn near flew to her car. I waited until she was inside and backing out of the driveway to close the door.

Charlie White was good for my weary soul. Charlie White was bad for me.

Knight: k.carver@gmail.com

Knight: It wasn't weird by the way. Maybe a little weird. But cute.

I'd reread Knight's text messages so many times since he sent them yesterday it was ridiculous! Even now as I waited for my mom to meet me for lunch on my break I was staring at the texts. She was late, and I was taking full advantage of being alone by rereading Knight's text messages. He was so handsome. So handsome. And sweet. And protective. And caring. But there was something about him that told me to stay away. Something that said he wasn't as good as he seemed.

Maybe he was.

Maybe he was the bad boy that knew how to be a good man to his woman.

But he just wasn't the bad boy for me.

I sent my mom a text asking where she was before sitting my phone down and looking over the menu yet again. This was one of the things I loved about working at Bundled. I could take an hour or two for lunch and not have to worry about anyone bothering me about it. I pretty much ran the place. Linda was the general manager, but I was the one that was in control. With me having that position, I never wanted it. I never wanted to be assistant or general manager; it just made sense for me to be promoted because I was doing all the work.

I refused to do all the work without the pay so I took the management position, but in all honesty... I was *so* ready to quit. My phone vibrated, but I was surprised to see Knight's name and a text message.

Knight: I'm at the gym. Are you ok?

Confused as to why he was texting me, I scrolled up and almost threw my heart up. I was so wrapped up in reading his texts that I sent the text to him instead of my mom! How in the hell was I supposed to explain that without looking crazier than I probably already did?

Before I could text back, Knight was calling me. I jumped in my seat and threw my phone onto the table softly before declining the call. Why would I decline the call? I'd just freaking texted him! Uh! With a deep breath, I picked my phone up and called him back.

"Charlie?"

God, his *voice*. His voice was so smooth and decadent. How could a voice be decadent? I don't know but his was. His voice was as decadent as a German chocolate cake. Rich. Deep. Dark. Sweet. Heavenly. Just... good.

"Charlie?"

"Huh? Hi."

"Are you OK?"

"I'm good. I meant to text my mom and sent it to you. My bad."

"So that means either you were reading my text messages or you were about to text me. Which one was it?"

My mouth dropped in surprise as I pushed and pulled my napkin back and forth on the table with the tips of my fingers.

"What makes you think either of those are the case?"

"What other reason would you have to be in my text thread, Charlie? You wanted to talk to me. You were thinking about me. Just admit it."

"Fine."

"Say it."

"I will not."

"Why not?"

Why not? Maybe because I didn't want to admit it. I didn't even want to admit that I didn't want to admit it!

"Knight..."

"I've been thinking about you too. I've been wanting to talk to you too. Does that help?"

"Yes," I almost whispered as I closed my eyes and pulled in a deep breath.

"I eased your mind. Ease mine."

"I was reading your texts while I waited for my mom. I have been thinking about you and wanting to talk to you."

"I didn't even send you anything worth saving. I can change that right now, though."

"Knight... that's really not necessary," he didn't answer me. "Knight..."

"Hold on. I'm texting you."

"Knight..."

Seconds passed before he answered, and when he did my phone chimed because of his incoming text.

"Yea?"

"Did you really just text me?"

"I sure did," I giggled as I crossed my legs and shook my head. "You said you're waiting for your mom?"

"Yea, she's meeting me while I'm on my lunch break."

"And what are you doing for dinner?"

"Eh... oh... um..."

"Don't worry, Charlie. I'm not asking you out on a date. If I ask you out on a date it will not be over the phone."

I didn't know if I should've been offended or flattered, so I remained silent until I caught sight of my mom's car pulling up.

"My mom is pulling up."

"Cool. Talk to you later."

"OK. Bye."

He ended the call and I quickly pulled up the text he'd sent.

Knight: You have a beautiful soul. I'm looking forward to exploring every part of you.

Holding a squeal in, I pressed my thighs together tightly as I texted him back.

That was sweet. Much better than calling me a little weird.

Knight: Lol. I like your weirdness. It's refreshing. Never hide it from me. Enjoy your mom. You'll be hearing from me soon.

My mom kissed my temple before sitting across from me. Hearing from him soon? No. That's not how this works. We weren't supposed to be communicating. I wasn't supposed to hear from him unless it was concerning Harlem. Other than that, we had an entire month to go before I started spending time with him. No. With Harlem. Time with Harlem. Not Knight.

"Well who has your attention?" my mom pried, causing me to put my phone down and give her my attention.

"Nobody. I was just thinking about a new client. How are you?"

"I'm good. Have you ordered yet?"

"Not yet. I was waiting for you."

She nodded and picked her menu up.

"I'm assuming you haven't quit or put in your two weeks' notice have you?"

Why did I expect her to wait before digging right in?

"No, Ma. I haven't done either yet."

She put her menu down and looked at me.

"Why not, Lie? Your business is doing great. Imagine how great it could be doing if you were able to focus on it fulltime. You already bring in more from that than you do at Bundled. You can make what you make at Bundled in one month on one client with your business. What are you waiting for, baby?"

"I just feel bad. They need me…"

Her head shook adamantly and I stopped talking.

"Don't go there. You are replaceable. You're a great worker, the best I'm sure they've ever had. You give your everything at Bundled. You put your heart into that store like it's your business, but it's not. Your business is suffering because you're devoting so much of your time putting money in someone else's pocket.

If I taught you all anything it was the importance of being your own person. Being your own boss. Your siblings took the leap and started their own businesses. Your father and I have our own businesses. You're the most creative out of us all. You read people well. They cling to you. You have the kind of spirit that makes people feel safe and comfortable. There's no doubt in my mind that anything you set your mind to you can conquer. What are you waiting for? Don't let having a good heart make you stagnant. Your position there isn't guaranteed, and to be honest, your purpose isn't either; not if you don't step fully into your destiny. Stop walking around with that letter of resignation in your purse. Turn it in."

Ending the conversation, she picked up her menu and made sure I couldn't see her face behind it.

"Linda, can I talk to you?" I asked as soon as I walked back into Bundled.

I didn't wait for her to answer as I made my way straight to the back of the store and into her office. If I was going to quit it had to be now. Now while I had the desire and courage to quit. After letting myself inside of her office, I sat down and replayed as much of my mother's words over in my head as I could.

She was right – my family hustled. We all had hustler spirits. We never expected anything to be handed to us. We understood that anything we wanted we had to go out and get. I guess that's why people like Bianca irritated me so much.

Linda came into her office and I was sitting there with my hands together in my lap. My usual smile was gone. I needed her to know that I meant business and wouldn't fold. No matter how hard she made leaving for me.

"What's wrong, lady?"

Her hand cupped my shoulder as she looked down at me with a face full of concern.

"Please, sit, Linda," instead of sitting across from me she sat next to me. "Linda…"

I pulled my two weeks' notice out of my purse and handed it to her. Linda read over it, her facial expression changing about four times before she finished. She placed the letter in her lap, let out a sigh, and ran her hand down her face.

"Charlie, you know how important you are to this company, but I won't try to guilt you into staying. I know that your business is doing well. I don't fault you at all for wanting to go fulltime. I'm going to miss you around here like hell and you and your work ethic will definitely be missed, but you have my full support."

My mouth opened slightly in shock. I was expecting more of a fight from her, but I would most certainly take this.

"Wow. OK. That was easy."

"I know you've been wanting to quit for a while. I heard you going over your speech the other day in my office, not to mention the fact that you doodled *I can't wait to quit* on a napkin like a million times two weeks ago and missed the garbage can when you threw it away. I've been preparing myself for you to leave."

I couldn't help but laugh. Of course my uncoordinated behind missed the trash can.

"Thank you for being so understanding, Linda. This was a very hard thing for me to do, but I know it's for the best."

"I agree. You're family here, and we all want to see family succeed. Anything you need I'm here, and feel free to leave your flyers and package sheets here. We'll continue to support you."

"Thank you. I appreciate that."

She pulled me in for a hug and we went back out to the floor, and I can't even lie... I felt a thousand pounds lighter.

⇒ KNIGHT ⇐

Ever since my mom passed, I've been making donations to Fuller hospital on her behalf. She didn't trust my father to do right by the money, so that was the only thing she asked me to do in her will. Every year at the start of their charity week I was supposed to donate ten thousand dollars until the money ran out. Even when the money she put aside in her insurance policy ran out I'd continue to honor her request with my money.

This year her doctor, Doctor Myers, threw some salt in the game. When I visited him to give him the check he asked me to be more hands on with the help this year. I tried to talk myself out of it by telling him that I'd much rather be a sponsor and donator and not a volunteer for any of the actual events, but he gave me a long, dramatic spill about how him and the rest of the board members would greatly appreciate my service.

So here I am – wasting a perfectly good Wednesday morning in a room full of people that I don't know or care to know waiting for Doctor Myers and whoever else to come in here and tell me what they need from me. Ignoring the small talk going on around me, I sent Carmen an 8ball request as I heard the door open and close. I had no intentions of looking up to see who it was until her scent hit my nose.

Charlie.

I looked up from my phone and sure enough, it was the beauty. She looked beautiful as always. Her eyes scanned the room briefly before landing on mine, and when they did she smiled widely and looked at the seat next to me. Like I'd want her to sit anywhere else. I patted the seat and she hung her head to conceal her smile as she came and sat next to me.

"What are you doing here?" I asked as she pulled her purse from her shoulder and sat it on the floor in front of her legs.

That was the first time I'd really paid any attention to the tattoo on her wrist. It looked like three sets of numbers.

"I was summoned by Dr. Berry. What about you?"

"Dr. Myers."

"This must be your first year participating? I don't remember seeing you at any of the events in the past."

"Yea. Usually I just write a check and that's about it."

"How's Harlem?"

"She's good. How are you?"

"I guess that was kind of rude, huh?" she giggled and fluffed her hair. "How are you too?"

"I'm good, Charlie."

"Me too."

I shook my head and smiled as I looked at the move Carmen made in poker. After making my move I put my phone in my lap and looked Charlie over. I didn't realize how deep I'd gotten in my stare until she looked at me and smiled.

"You stare at me a lot," she observed.

"Does that bother you?"

Her legs crossed and she lowered her head as she played with the strap of her sandal.

"Not necessarily," her eyes returned to mine as she licked her lips. "I'm just not used to it."

"You're not used to a man staring at you? I find that hard to believe, Charlie."

Her small, delicate hand squeezed my forearm as she smiled and made no effort to remove it. And I was glad she didn't.

"They do, but… it's just different with you."

"How so?"

She pulled her hand back to herself and sighed.

"When they look at me it's like they're just... looking at me, but when you look at me... it feels like..." she paused and tilted her head as she looked into my eyes. "Like you're looking through me. In me. Why?"

I didn't answer her right away. I wanted to give myself time to answer her question right. The last thing I wanted to do was fly too deep because of my fast. I didn't want her to think that there was a chance for something to pop off between us when there wasn't, but I wanted to be as honest and open with her as I possibly could.

"There's something about you that I know. Something that's familiar yet new. I can't explain it I just... there's something about you that I feel attached to. So yea, I stare at you because you're beautiful, but I guess I'm also trying to figure out what it is about you that..."

I shook my head as I scratched the top of it. How could I explain something to her that I hadn't even figured out myself?

"Maybe I just have a common face," she reasoned with a shrug.

"There's nothing about your face that's common, Charlie," Charlie blushed and covered her face with her hands. I took her by the wrist and pulled her left hand down.

"What's this tattoo about?"

Now that I was looking closely I could see that it was three dates. She ran her fingers across the dates and sighed as the door opened. Doctor Myers along with three other doctors that I didn't know walked in.

"So sorry to keep you guys waiting. For those of you who don't know me, I'm Dr. Berry. You're here because you all have agreed to help us with the charity events coming up later this summer. We're hoping to have all of the details worked out by the end of this month with your help so we can start promoting and networking at the start of next month. Ideally we'd like to have our charity week the last week of May. Today is all about brainstorming. Any fresh and new fundraising ideas that you all can come up with will be greatly appreciated. I have to step out, but I just wanted to thank you all and let you know that you are greatly appreciated."

Doctor Berry tipped his head, then locked eyes with Charlie. She waved and he smiled as he returned the gesture. He looked at me and his smile fell, but he quickly recovered and left the room.

I was not expecting to see Knight at this volunteer meeting, but the sight of him was a very pleasant surprise. Knight was different. He made no effort to try and hide his attraction to me, but he didn't act on it in any way.

So far in our 30-minute meeting we'd decided that Alvin was over entertainment. Crystal was over the food. Tracy and Olivia were over raffles, networking, and taking care of reservations, tickets, and everything like that. Derrick was the treasurer. The only people who didn't have any responsibilities yet were Knight and I, which meant we were over coming up with the nightly events.

He and I had moved to a table in the back of the conference room and had a piece of paper between us. We were close for whatever reason, and every time he spoke the smell of the mint on his breath and movement of his lips made me want to kiss him.

We needed to come up with this list of events quick!

"I think we definitely should have at least two sporting events," Knight suggested. "Most of the sponsors over the years have been old white men. I think we should have a golf tournament for them, and a basketball game for the younger men. We can charge to play and attend the events. And throughout take more donations. Maybe have a set price that the winners will have to pay and the losers will have to pay at the end."

"That's a really good idea."

I wrote his ideas down and bit my bottom lip to conceal my smile as I looked back at him. "Two down three more to go," with the pen on my cheek I looked towards the ceiling in thought, but there was no avoiding the way his eyes roamed my face, neck, and chest. Self-consciously, I grabbed the collar of my shirt as I looked at him again. I hated for anyone to see my scar; especially men. That's why 90 percent of the shirts in my wardrobe were button downs or shirts that came up to my neck. "What do you think about ending the week with a gala? We can sell tickets to attend. I went to a function last year that sold their tickets for five hundred each. Eight for couples."

"That's a good idea. Give a brotha a chance to get dapper."

He popped his invisible collar and I laughed louder than I planned on. Eyes were on me as conversations stopped, and before I could even say anything the look Knight gave them made them turn away from us. When his face softened he returned his attention to me.

"That was so corny, Knight. Did you really just say dapper and pop your collar? What year is this? 2000?"

"Whatever, Charlie. Just write the shit down."

He put my hand on top of the paper and I laughed again; this time as quietly as I possibly could.

"Maybe we could also have a game night. Oh! Or Casino night. There won't be a charge to get in the door, but instead of leaving with their winnings everyone will donate their winnings to the hospital."

"Charlie, that's a damn good idea. I have no doubt that that's going to be the biggest money maker. Gambling is the quickest way to spend money without a thought. That's definitely a good idea."

I blushed as I wrote it down.

"OK, so now we only need one more event. Any ideas?"

The sly smile that covered his face worried me. And when he didn't let me in on what he was thinking right away I was even more alarmed.

"Knight…"

"Hear me out before you say no."

"…Oookay."

"I think we should do an auction."

My skeptical face made him chuckle.

"What's so bad about that?"

"I was thinking we could auction…" he looked around the room and smiled. "You."

"What? Knight…"

His hand covered mine, and the act made me shut up completely.

"You are the most beautiful being I've ever seen in my life. Not just physically, but your spirit is beautiful, Charlie. You have this loving and positive vibe that's contagious. If you were to stand on stage we'd make millions, beauty."

Giving me time to register what he'd just said, Knight paused and rested more on the table. In this position we were face to face instead of side by side. His face was less than six inches away from mine. I could literally feel every slow breath he took. Fighting the urge to run my fingers across his face, I sat on my free hand.

I don't know if his plan was to distract me and make me agree, or if he honestly had no idea what being this close to him was doing to me, but whatever the case, I didn't plan on asking him to move back.

"This is what I'm thinking – instead of having multiple women to bid on there will only be one," he smiled and lowered his head briefly before pulling his eyes back to mine. "Because there's only one you. All of the bets will be accepted and donated, but only the highest bidder will win a date with you."

Since he still had one hand covering mine on the table, I used the free one that I was sitting on to scratch my eyebrow. I wasn't insecure… but… I mean… I really didn't have the time to date, but I also had no *desire* to date. The last time I went out and started to really like a guy he bruised my heart and crushed my soul. After that I just… invested my time and energy in other areas of my life.

I didn't want to waste time getting to know a man, falling for him, exposing myself to him, and then dealing with his rejection when he saw me. *Really* saw me. It was just easier to not deal with men at all. At least on that level.

"Knight, you said some really, really sweet things, but… honestly I'm just not comfortable with that. I haven't dated in years and I kind of want to keep it like that."

The confusion that covered his face made me smile.

"You haven't gone out on a date in years?"

"Nope. I have one nice guy friend that I hang out with from time to time. We've known each other since middle school. When he's single and I need male companionship we kick it, but that's about it."

"Why not?"

"Why not what?"

"Don't you date?"

Not wanting to go into detail about it, I pulled my hand from under his and put them both in my lap. Sensing my apprehension, he nodded.

"OK. We don't have to go there. Do you trust me, Charlie? I know we haven't known each other long bu-"

"Yes."

Knight smiled softly as his palm cupped my cheek. His thumb caressed my cheek and I swear I shivered as my eyes closed and opened.

"If you trust me… trust that I won't allow you to be put in a position that will make you uncomfortable, nor will I allow you to be with a man that would do anything to make you uncomfortable or feel disrespected or violated. Leave all of the details to me and I promise you'll be at ease. Just commit to this for me. Or at least commit to thinking about it. I don't want you to do anything you're not comfortable with. You know what, just forget it. We can do a silent auction instead."

He sat right in his seat and started to write that on the list, but I put my hand over his and stopped him. I wasn't completely sure how this was going to work out, but I did trust him, and it was a good idea, and it would be nice to have men pine over me, and you know what… fuck it.

"I'm down."

⋛ KNIGHT ⋚

Before I took Harlem to the doctor I went to the gym. The goal was to release the tension and nervous energy before we got to the doctor, but when we arrived and she told me that *Tage* said he was on his way I got irritated all over again.

I reached out to him and told him that I wanted to meet with him and his parents, and he told me that he'd stop by, but he didn't want his parents to know about the baby. Although I respected his honesty, I couldn't respect his decision, so I told Harlem that his ass didn't need to be here today.

If he was man enough to plant those seeds he needed to be man enough to not only water and nurture them but acknowledge them also. I refused to allow him to give my sister anything less than the respect and support she deserved.

When she told me that he was coming I couldn't even be mad at him. I was irritated with her. I was irritated with her because she was starting a dangerous cycle of letting him do this shit halfway. If he kept her a secret from his parents, I figured he'd keep her a secret from other girls too. Then I started getting paranoid thinking about her moving in with him and him cheating and lying and being disrespectful and not bringing anything to the table but his dick and I just was about to flip the fuck out.

Since she hadn't been called back yet, I stepped outside and called Charlie. I figured she might be at work and wouldn't answer, but I'd settle for hearing her voicemail. To my surprise and delight she answered.

"Hi," she spoke, and I could hear the smile in her voice.

"You busy?"

"Nah."

"You at work?"

"Yes, but I can talk."

Leaning against the wall, I scratched the top of my head and sighed.

"Her little friend is on his way up here."

"I thought you said he couldn't come?"

"I did."

She chuckled and the sound of it made me smile even though I didn't want to.

"Are you going to be nice, Knight? Or do I need to come up there to play referee?"

"I'll try, but I can't make any promises. That's why I called you. You make me feel better."

I'd said it before I knew it, but I didn't regret it. It was the truth. She *did* make me feel better.

"I do?"

"You do."

"What are we doing, Knight?"

"What do you mean?"

"We shouldn't be talking as much as we are. This is dangerous."

"What's dangerous about it, Charlie?"

She sighed into the phone, giving me the time to lock eyes with a youngin' as he walked towards the office. He looked like a Tage. Long, curly hair all on his head pulled up in a bun like a female.

"Charlie, I think he's here. I'll call you back."

Without waiting for her to OK that I disconnected the call and followed him into the office. Sure enough he made his way over to Harlem. She looked up at him and rolled her eyes before looking towards the door for me. I made my way over to them and looked from him to her.

Harlem stood and stepped between us. She placed her hand on my stomach and pushed me back slightly.

"Knight, this is Tage. Tage, this is Knight."

I scratched my neck and looked him over as he placed his hands in his pockets.

"You tell your parents about my sister and the baby?"

"Uh, not yet."

"Then there's no reason for you to be here."

"Knight…"

I pulled Harlem behind me and stepped closer to him.

"I'm not going to play with you. I told you what you had to do if you wanted to be a part of this. Until you tell your parents there's no point of you coming around. You need to leave."

"Knight!" Harlem grabbed my arm and turned me towards her. "He has more of a right to be here than you! You can't make him leave!"

"Do you hear yourself, Harlem? This nigga ain't claiming you or this kid, but you think I'm about to let him stick around to find out what you're having? What I tell you about giving a nigga the world for free? He will *never* pay you for it. Do not settle for this. Make him earn his place in you and your child's life."

"I don't have time for this shit," he mumbled as he walked away. "Call me when he ain't around and let me know what's up, Harlem."

And with that he walked out of the office. She put all of her strength into punching my chest before pressing her face into it and wrapping her arms around my waist as she cried frustrated tears. I wrapped my arms around her and kissed the top of her head.

"It's OK, sweetheart. I got you."

"I hate you so much for that, Knight. Why didn't you just let him stay? He'll tell them eventually. I want my baby to have both parents around. It's bad enough that we won't be in the same house. I at least want him to be around," she removed herself from my chest when the nurse called her name. Harlem wiped her face and glared at me. "I really don't like you right now, Knight. When we leave here, you need to get me Charlie. I don't want you coming to any more appointments. I can't believe you did that to me."

She walked away and I was tempted to just wait for her in the car since it was obvious she didn't want me involved, but I promised to be here for her, so I sucked it up and followed behind her.

With no idea if Charlie was still at work or not, I looked around the parking lot for her car before I parked. When I found it I parked next to it and went into the store. She was nowhere on the floor, so I had one of the cashiers to call her. When she came out and saw me she smiled. I tried to return it... but it was hard.

As if she knew I needed one, she wrapped her arms around my neck and pulled me into her for a hug. Her arms stayed around my neck for a few seconds before she dropped them to my waist and pulled me closer. Her gripping me as tightly as I held her made me groan and run my lips against her neck.

Charlie shivered and grabbed two handfuls of my shirt before pulling away. She let me go, but I didn't let go of her. Not until I looked down at her and her beauty had my dick growing. I didn't want the feel of it to make her uncomfortable, so I released her and took a step back.

"So... how did it go? Is everything all right?" she inquired as she grabbed my hand and led me to the bench I sat on the first time I came here.

"She's mad at me. She told me to do whatever it took to get you to start working with her now because she doesn't want me involved anymore since I made him leave."

Her face softened as she grabbed my hand and pulled it into her lap.

"She'll get over it. It may be years from now but she will. She doesn't understand that you're trying to make him man up now, but when she does I bet she'll thank you for it."

"Will you start this month? I'm willing to pay whatever extra I have to. She has a tendency to run away when things aren't going her way and I don't want her doing that while she's pregnant."

"Sure. And you don't have to worry about paying anything extra. I'll be done working here soon so I'll need something to do with my free time."

"You're leaving?"

"Yep. Put in my two weeks' notice a few days ago. I'm gonna go fulltime with my business."

"That's great, beauty. I'm really proud of you. I'm sure you'll do great."

She blushed and held my hand a little tighter.

"What is she having?"

"A boy."

"Even more reason for you to want him to do right, huh?"

"Exactly."

"She'll come around. Don't worry yourself. I know that's easier for me to say than it is for you to do, but... try."

"I will. I don't want to hold you. I just wanted to stop by and see if you'd start early."

"You don't have to rush out. I'm on my lunch break."

"Have you eaten anything?"

"No. Not yet."

"Then let's grab something."

"Knight..."

"It's not a date. Trust me, that's the last thing on my list of priorities right now too."

She thought about it for a few seconds then agreed.

"Cool. Let me grab my purse, then we can head out."

I nodded and watched her ass as she walked away. That was the truth; I wasn't looking to date or be in a relationship right now. My fast was still intact. I just... wanted to spend every possible moment that I could with her.

Charlie

Today was my first day working with Harlem, and it caught me totally and completely by surprise when she was sitting outside on the porch waiting for me. Yea, I knew her and Knight were having a little static between the two of them, but I thought they'd be over it by now. Her doctor's appointment had been three days ago. I definitely wasn't expecting them to still be at odds.

There was no need for me to cut my car off because as soon as she me pulling into the driveway she stood and started walking towards the car. When she got in she leaned over the middle console and hugged my neck – surprising the heck out of me!

"Hey, Charlie," she muttered as she sat back in her seat and put on her seatbelt.

"Hey, sweetheart. What's wrong?"

Her head shook at the same time her bottom lip poked out.

"Do you mind if I go speak to Knight before we leave?"

Her head shook again. I got out and walked up to the front door. Since it was still open I knocked softly then stepped inside.

"Knight?" I don't know why I even called out for him. As quietly as I did it he wouldn't be able to hear me. "Knight?" I repeated a little louder as I walked down the hallway.

Knight was sitting in the middle of his couch. Elbows on his thighs. Face in his palms. Something must have happened today. With small, soft steps I walked until I was standing in front of him. He didn't look up, but he knew I was there because he inhaled deeply and acknowledged…

"You always smell so good," before wrapping his arms around my waist, pulling me even closer, and resting his head on my breasts.

The act made me lock up immediately out of fear of him feeling my scar, but I put my own feelings aside to tend to his.

"What's wrong, Knight?"

With no answer from him, I got on my knees before him. My hands went to his thighs as he tried to avoid my eyes. That didn't last very long. For the first time since I'd known him, my hair was pulled back into a ponytail, so he had a very good look at my face today.

Knight smiled and ran his pointing finger across my cheek.

"And you're so fucking beautiful."

I blushed and squeezed his thighs.

"I did not come in here to be complimented. I came in here to check on you. What happened?"

"Nothing. She just made it very clear that I wasn't allowed to be involved today like the petty betty that she is, and I told her that Page couldn't be involved either, and that turned into another back and forth match that I don't even do. Then she went outside to wait for you."

"His name is Tage, Knight. You know that."

He smiled and ran his middle finger down my neck. If the chills weren't enough to make me pull away, the sight of the desire in his eyes was... but for some reason... I couldn't move.

"I really need you to get off your knees, Charlie."

"Why?"

Knight's head shook as his eyes lowered to my breasts, and before I knew it his hands were cupping my face and his lips were almost on mine. As much... and trust me... I wanted to kiss him a lot... but as much as I wanted to kiss him... I just couldn't. I got all weird about it as usual and scooted away from him on my palms and feet.

"I'm sorry," he mumbled running his hand over his face as he lowered it.

"No it's fine it's just... kisses lead to touching and touching leads to... you know..."

"Sex?"

I nodded and sat flat on the floor.

"I wasn't thinking about sex, Charlie. Not right now anyway."

"But you have?"

"How could I not? You're beautiful and I adore you. I just... I'm feeling like shit and needed... I don't know."

"You adore me?"

His eyes returned to mine.

"I adore you," as soon as I opened my mouth to respond he cut me off. "You should go. She's waiting for you and... I don't want to turn this into something it's not."

"Are you dismissing me?"

Knight stood and headed for the kitchen. When he made it next to me he looked down and said, "I'm not dismissing you, I'm protecting you."

"Protecting me from what?"

"Me."

"But what does that mean?"

"Just go, Charlie."

I stood and followed him into the kitchen. My hand went into his as I turned him to face me. On the tips of my toes I kissed his forehead. Both eyes. His nose. Both cheeks. The corners of his mouth. I could tell he wanted to wrap his arms around me and keep me close because his arms went from the sides of him, to behind his back, and ended with his hands on top of his head.

"I know that's probably not the kiss you wanted but... I hope it makes you feel at least a little better."

He put some space between us and turned to the side.

"It was perfect. Go."

The ride to the store was silent. All I could do was think about Knight and what he said. That he was protecting me from him. What the hell did that even mean? What could he possibly need to protect me from within him? Should it even matter? I should just… take that warning and that protection and just… stay away.

Harlem started to loosen up when we started shopping. Everything she wanted I made a list of and preordered it. I gave Brea a little cut of my profit for filling my orders for me when she got off work. All I would have to do is pick everything up in the morning when the store opened and set it up for Harlem.

After shopping at Bundled we went to Babies R Us and this cute little boutique just outside of Memphis that I absolutely love! They have the cutest nursery furniture! She wanted his approval. We ended up having to wait a few minutes just for him to OK her choices before we could even place the order.

I thought she'd be tired and ready to go home after that, but she wanted to stop for lunch, so we went to O'Charley's to grab a bite to eat before I took her home. Harlem intrigued me. From her looks, to her spunky little attitude, and her hunger for independence no matter how dependent life or her actions made her. I wanted to know about her, but I didn't want to be all up in her business, so I tried to make the conversation as light as I possibly could.

"Soooo tell me about you, Harlem."

She stopped buttering her roll long enough to look at me and smile softly before returning her attention to it.

"Um, there's not much to tell. I'm 16 and pregnant. I go to Kirby High School. I'm the youngest in my family," her smile started to fade. "My mom died when I was six. After that the rest of my family kind of just... fell apart," her smile was completely gone. "You know about my brother Knight, and we also have a sister. Carmen."

"I know that Knight travels a lot because of his job. How does that work with you living with him?"

"Well, I don't really live with him. I guess I do now. I don't think he's going to let me go anywhere any time soon," her smile returned. "I was staying with my dad, but when I told him that I was pregnant he basically told me if I wanted to stay I had to have an abortion, so I left. I called Knight and he came home and I've been with him ever since."

"And you said your sister doesn't live in Memphis?"

Harlem shook her head as she chewed a piece of her bread.

"No. She moved to Atlanta for college and never came back. I don't blame her because I wanted to do the same thing, but it doesn't look like I'll be able to," she put the roll down and placed her hands on the sides of her plate.

"I know it probably looks like I'm ungrateful and difficult for no reason. I know I probably look... because Knight is doing so much for me. He paid for you. Paying for all of my baby's stuff. Letting me stay with him.

And I love him and appreciate him I really do it's just... I hate that he thinks he can just come back to Memphis during his off season and control my life. Like... I've been raising myself practically since momma died. Daddy ain't do shit for me but keep a roof over my head and take care of my necessities. I did everything else.

I taught myself how to cook. I washed my hair and braided it into pigtails until I was taught by Princess's mother how to do more. I cleaned the house and did my laundry. I was doing that shit at eight. Yea, I fucked up and got pregnant, but it wasn't because I've been out here living reckless every day of my life.

I slipped up one time one time and… and he thinks he can just come in and take control and it just irritates me. It makes me want to do the opposite of whatever he says."

Her elbows went to the table and she palmed her face. I remained silent for a good little while to make sure she was done before I spoke.

"I know you love him. I know you appreciate him. But I'm sure it would make him feel better to hear you say it. We need to figure out how to make this work. He loves you, Harlem, and he only wants what's best for you and the baby. Would it make it easier for you to do as he said if he didn't try to force you to? If he maybe suggested things to you instead of presenting them as demands?"

She scratched her head with one hand and rubbed her eye with the other.

"Yes. I always listen to him. I'd listen now if he was just nicer about it."

"I think that's understandable. You are a minor living in his home, but you're about to be a mom too. So he has to find that balance of protecting you and taking care of you like he wants to, but giving you the space to take care of yourself and the baby. Why don't you just tell him everything that you told me? I think he'll understand."

"What's up with you two?"

"What's up with who two?"

Harlem smiled and picked her roll back up.

"You and Knight, Charlie. Don't play."

I eyed our waitress as she made her way over to us to take our order. Seeing her gave me the perfect excuse to not answer Harlem right away. Quite frankly, I didn't know what to say. We placed our orders – low country shrimp for me and chicken tenders for her – then the waitress left and Harlem's attention was back on me.

"There's nothing up with us. Why? Did he say there was something up with us?"

"He doesn't have to. I know there is."

"How do you know?"

"By the way he looks at you," she sat up in her seat and leaned into the table, causing me to do the same. As if she was about to whisper a secret to me that no one else was allowed to hear. "We all handled losing my mother in different ways. Carmen left. I rebel. My daddy and Knight they both shut down.

Daddy shut down with everyone, but Knight really just doesn't let anyone new in. I guess he doesn't want to lose anyone else that he loves. He keeps his family close enough to make sure we're straight... but it's like... he's detached himself enough to not be too bothered if he lost us.

I don't know. I can't explain it. It's like... he'll be messed up if anything happens to us, but it's like he expects to lose us. I guess he's prepared for lost now. I don't know. But he doesn't get to know new people and he really doesn't commit to women.

Now don't get me wrong, he dates a lot of them, and I've disapproved of everyone that I've known of but you... I just see it in the way he looks at you. He likes you. And that's saying a lot. There's something about you that's just... so familiar and necessary. Makes us feel comfortable.

Knight doesn't like to feel. That's what it is. He doesn't like to feel. Losing momma made him not want to love and feel. But since you've been around I can tell he's pulling out of that. You make him feel. You give him something he can feel. He needs that. He needs you. We both do."

Speechless. That's what I was. Speechless. I picked up a roll and bit into it because I had absolutely nothing to say.

⟩ KNIGHT ⟨

Had I known inviting a few of my old homies and some of the players from the team was going to turn into such a huge gathering in the middle of the day I wouldn't have invited them. It was my intention to invite the team and my friends to get them to participate in the charity basketball game and golf tournament.

We all met at Roman's Lounge for a drink at the bar, and after they all finished calling their people to come out the lounge was full and they were straight up going live and getting full of it like it was a Saturday night. It was cool, but that wasn't my scene anymore. Even when I went out with the team when we were on the road I'd always have my own little section in the back of VIP where I could chill, but as long as they didn't expect me to cover the tab we wouldn't have any problems.

I was at the left end of the bar talking to two of the men that I knew for sure would participate when our waitress came over yet again to *check on us*. I've never been the type to judge, but I could tell just by the way she was dressed that she used her place of employment as a means to meet men. Men she thought could benefit her financially or sexually.

When I first got here she immediately hopped on me, but when the team started floating in her attention went elsewhere. Either they told her that they were here for me and she thought I had money, or she wasn't getting the play she thought she would because she was returning her attention to me.

Instead of keeping some distance between us when she asked, she squeezed in between Edward and I and made sure her body was as close to mine as she could possibly get it. There was no way for me to avoid brushing up against her when I turned to face her, and the moment I did she smiled.

"I was just making sure you didn't need anything else from me, otherwise I was going to go ahead and see how you wanted to handle the check."

"I'm good. I'm paying for my drinks only. See everybody else about their own."

"Your face is familiar. Are you on the team with them?"

Her hand found its way to my knee. I was tempted to tell her ass to get from 'round me, but I didn't want to embarrass her. I didn't want her to think she had a chance with me either, so I didn't even look down at her hand.

"Nah," I answered dryly.

She wasn't bad looking just way too thirsty. Besides, I had Charlie to play with. There was nothing this waitress or anyone else could do to pull my attention away from Charlie.

Charlie.

I needed to talk to her about yesterday. Kissing her... yea kissing her had definitely been something I thought about a lot. I never considered acting on it, and the way she reacted let me know I never would. I had to put my growing desire for her aside. I don't want to do anything to make her uncomfortable. For the next five months she's going to have to be around for Harlem. I don't need her trying to quit or anything like that because she thinks I can't handle myself around her.

To be honest, I'd never had that type of problem with a woman before. Most of the time they made the first move, and when I did it was made knowing full well that they wanted it to happen just as much as I wanted it to happen. I don't know what had gotten into me. I guess it was just her being her and being so caring and present and sweet and on her knees looking up at me like I was a King and...

"Oh. Well. OK. Um... do you come here a lot? I usually work the night shift, but I've never seen you in here before."

Scratching my forehead, I inhaled deeply and sighed.

"Nah. I don't come here often at all, baby girl."

She didn't take my brush off seriously. Not seriously at all.

"Oh. I wish you would. Seeing you would make my shifts fly by a lot easier."

I didn't think it was possible for her to get closer to me, but she did, and her hand sliding up my thigh had my legs opening naturally. My dick was definitely proving it had a mind of its own as it grew. I was fasting. No sex. Really, I wasn't even supposed to be calling and texting women, but Charlie made me happily break that rule.

"Is that right?"

"Right."

"I'll see what I can do."

She smiled and bit down on her lip as she put some space between us.

"Cool. I'll put my number on the back of your receipt."

I nodded and watched as she walked away and went behind the bar.

"Dude, what the hell is wrong with you? She was practically throwing you the pussy and you didn't bite," Edward said in disbelief.

"Man, just as easily as she threw it at me is just as easily as she threw it at somebody else in here I'm sure."

"Whatever. You could've at least gotten her to head you up."

I looked over at Edward and shook my head.

"At what cost? I'm trying to cleanse myself of these females not add on more. I don't need her calling me and texting me and expecting shit from me that I don't have to give. I'm good on that."

"What happened to the Knight that I know? The Knight that I know would've taken her to the bathroom and handled that immediately."

I shrugged and watched as the waitress made her way back over to me with my receipt and a smile. I don't know where that Knight was. Even with me fasting, if a woman was easy enough I'd just fall and get back up on the next day, but this day... I had no desire to entertain her or anyone else.

For the first time in I think my entire adult life I was more content with whatever this was that I had with Charlie than having sex and that scared me. That scared me a lot. Even with that fear and uneasiness of what was happening to me, I couldn't wait to get home and see her. She was coming over to deliver the stuff she and Harlem purchased yesterday.

"Here's your receipt."

I looked at the waitress's name tag for the first time today.

"Cool. Thanks, Robin."

"No problem."

Robin winked and left. After letting everyone know that I was about to leave I pulled enough cash out of my wallet to cover my bill and give Robin a nice tip. Then I left the money, the receipt, and her number that was on the back of it on the top of the bar.

Walking into my house and hearing Harlem and Charlie laughing gave me this warm feeling in the pit of me that made it feel like I was walking into a home. With the thought that neither of them would be here forever, I made my way upstairs and into Harlem's temporary room. Charlie's eyes found mine first because she was facing the door, and when they did her laugh was turned into a quiet smile.

Harlem turned around and looked from my face to the packages of Ricki's cookies I'd picked up for her and Charlie as peace offerings when I left the lounge. I knew Harlem loved Ricki's soft baked cookies and I was hoping Charlie would too, or at least appreciate the fact that I grabbed her some along with Harlem.

"Hi," Charlie spoke softly.

"What's up?"

Her gaze lowered to the bag she was pulling stuff out of as she fought to pull her smile in.

"Can I talk to you?" Harlem asked as she stood.

"Me?"

"Yes you, boo."

"I'm back to boo?"

Harlem rolled her eyes and pushed me out of the doorway. She grabbed one of the packages of cookies from my hand and led the way downstairs. We went into the dining room and sat across from each other. I put the other package of cookies on the table as she began to speak.

"I would really like for you to put the baby's furniture and stuff up when it arrives, Knight."

"That would mean I'm involved, and you don't want me involved remember?"

"Don't be difficult when I'm trying to apologize!" she whined as she opened the box. After biting one of the cookies and keeping her eyes closed in sheer delight until she was done, Harlem continued. "I'm sorry for being... difficult. I know that you only said and did what you said and did because you love and care about me. And I really do appreciate you for that, Knight, but you have to let me make my own choices and mistakes. I don't want to resent you for anything. Let me walk this path on my own. I want you to walk it with me every step of the way, but I have to walk it on my own. I need you at my side, not in front of me forcing my every move. If Tage is a dog ass..."

"Watch your mouth."

"If Tage is no good, I need to find out on my own. I want your advice and help, but can you give it when I ask for it? Can you at least do that?"

I sat back in my seat and sighed as I considered her request.

"So you want me to just let you make bad decisions and only tell you it's a bad decision if you ask me to?"

"Yes. If I'm going to stay here…"

"You *are* staying here."

Her eyes rolled as she shook her head.

"If I'm going to stay here we have to have that boundary."

"Boundary? The hell you know about some damn boundaries?"

"Well, I was talking to Charlie and she suggested that I…"

"Charlie?"

"Yes. Charlie. She's the reason I'm even talking to you in the first place. I was just going to continue to be petty and ignore you and irritate you, but she suggested that I tell you how I felt. And that we create boundaries. Boundaries that will help you understand that I'm still your baby sister, but I'm also about to be a mother. I need to grow up and deal with some things on my own, Knight. And boundaries for me to help me remember that you love me and want what's best for me. So I promise to not flip and take everything so personally as an attack on my independence if you promise to lighten up and walk with me instead of in front of me."

"That's fair."

Harlem smiled as she stood and walked over to me. She gave me a hug and kiss before mushing my head and walking away.

"Thanks for the cookies. I love you."

"You better."

Well damn. My baby sister was growing up on me. Talking about independence and boundaries and respect. What did I expect? She'd practically started raising herself. I felt bad as hell about leaving her, but I felt like I couldn't be any good to her or anyone else. Not being there for mama filled me with so much guilt and anger. Made me feel like I couldn't be there for anyone else. But Harlem never held that against me or Carmen.

She never harbored any type of hate or anger or even resentment because we weren't there for her as much as we should have been when she was growing up. Yea, I stopped by whenever I was in town and I made sure she was straight financially. We talked at least every two days. But I wasn't *there*. Her heart wouldn't allow her to hold that against me, though, and for that I was grateful. And I planned on making up for my absence now.

Next up was Charlie. I returned to the door and asked to speak with her. She followed me to the dining room hesitantly – as if she was afraid that I had a problem with anything that she'd said to Harlem or something. Charlie tried to sit across from me in the same seat Harlem had, but I found myself wanting her closer. I grabbed her hand and sat her next to me.

Her hands were in her lap as her eyes shyly found mine.

"These are for you," I slid her the cookies and she smiled. "I'm not sure if you like these…"

"I love Ricki's cookies. You didn't have to get me anything, Knight, but thank you."

I nodded and thought over my words carefully.

"Listen, I just wanted to apologize again for yesterday. I'm not going to lie and say that I didn't want to kiss you, but I didn't plan on acting on that desire. I was feeling a way over Harlem and you being here and being all loving and positive… your energy… it transferred and took away the anger and uncertainty that I was feeling and I just… couldn't help myself."

"You don't have to apologize for that. Like at all. If I was a normal woman kissing you would've been the highlight of my life," she smiled and paused momentarily as her eyes lowered to my lips. "But my own personal issues are what made me react the way I did. It had absolutely nothing to do with you, Knight. I genuinely like you. You're handsome and sweet, but I get the feeling you have no problem taking control and laying down the law," the tip of her finger ran across the mole she called a beauty mark on my finger. "You're perfect."

I can't tell you how long we sat there like that, with her running her finger across mine, but we didn't stop until my doorbell sounded off. She removed her hand immediately and tried to stand, but my hand went to her waist and I sat her back down.

"Let them wait," I took her hands into mine and kissed them both. Her shoulders tensed and she tried to pull her hands away, but I didn't let her. "I don't know what guards you have up and why, and I can't even say if I'm up for the challenge of knocking them down. I can't say if I'm capable. What I can say is that I like you. A lot. And if all I have are these next five months to just stare at you and vibe with you… I will gladly accept that. Just promise me that you won't be scared of me, Charlie. Of what I feel for you. How I express those feelings. I'm not used to them… to feeling… and I honestly don't know what to do with them right now but… just don't let me run you away. OK?"

The sight of her eyes watering made my heart skip a beat. Literally. She closed them and inhaled deeply as she pulled me closer to her by our still connected hands. Charlie let go of mine only to wrap her arms around my neck for a hug.

I inhaled her scent as I hugged her waist. Pulling her as close as I could.

The doorbell rang again.

Neither of us made a move to release each other.

"I'm so scared," she whispered into my ear, and the feel of her tear hitting my neck snatched my words.

"Charlie..." was all that would come out as I tried to pull away but she held me closer. Tighter.

The front door opened and Harlem's squeal let me know it was her furniture. "Charlie..."

"Please. Just. Let me get myself together. Just hold me for a second."

"But I need to know why you're afraid. I need to know what you're afraid of so I can keep it from happening. What are you scared of, Charlie?"

She inhaled deeply and pulled away from me as she wiped her face. Charlie stood and turned her back to me as she looked at the delivery men taking boxes upstairs.

"Falling for you. I'm... scared of falling for you."

Her eyes met mine briefly before her feet started to move, and it felt like each step she took away from me somehow pulled her heart even closer to mine. Felt like each step she took away from me somehow made me want to chase after her. Not physically... but emotionally.

I had no idea how screwed up she was. How damaged she was. Maybe she was just as screwed up and damaged as me. Maybe that's why we got along and vibed as well as we did. Maybe that's why she was scared. Lord knows I didn't want to take it there with her. He knew I didn't want to get to know her. See her all vulnerable and exposed. Make her fall for me and trust me. Only for her to leave me or be left by me.

So why did He present her to me? Awaken me. Like she was my rib. The woman I'd been waiting for. The one created to fit me perfectly. Five months. She would be gone in five months. I'd be back on the road in six. And none of this would matter anymore.

Charlie

It was Deja, my beautiful yet crazy best friend of forever, who decided I needed a night out. She chose Sticks so we could play a little pool and have a couple of drinks. Today was my last day at Bundled, and she swore it wouldn't be official if I didn't go out and celebrate, so I decided to go and unwind with my bestie.

Deja and I have been best friends for as long as I've known myself. Like seriously. Like ever since I've known me I've known her. That's how close we are. She's the only person that knew just how sick I really was. She was the only person I allowed to see me cry and be in pain because of my condition. I didn't even show that to my parents.

We went on our first date together. Graduated together. Went to college together. With my surgery, I was forced to withdraw from school. Her crazy behind refused to graduate without me, so she graduated a year late just to be able to be in the same class as me.

Now that was love.

Crazy love.

But love.

Our drinks and game was forgotten when Ella Mai's "Down" began to play. She dropped her pool stick onto the table and we immediately started belting the song out.

"Tell me what you wanna feel? Is there something I can heal? We can paint a perfect picture, picture, make a story we can tell. Honestly I ain't tryna push. I just know where to look. See you watching me watching you watch my body don't be scared to speak up."

By now, we were standing in front of each other vibing out to the beat. Her hands went to my waist and mine were around her neck as we swayed to the beat.

"Wanna know if you're sure. Maybe I could be the cure."

She pulled me in for a hug and whispered…

"Lie, I think they think we're lesbians."

I laughed and pulled myself away from her, taking in the small crowd that had gathered around us.

"Don't really know what you do to me, but take that next stop boy that's cool with me. Cool with me."

"I think you're right, Day."

I grabbed my drink as she picked her pool stick back up. When the men that were watching us realized the show was over the crowd slowly began to fade. I giggled at some of the disappointed looks on their faces as the crowd cleared. My smile fell when my eyes landed on Knight. He was seated in the back with a woman practically hanging off of his body.

It was obvious that he wasn't as interested in her as she was in him, but that didn't cause him to put space between them. He must have felt someone looking at him because his eyes scanned the room until they landed on me.

"I just want you to myself. Tryna be the one that matter. Follow me let's make it clear."

His hand tightened around her hip before he patted it and pushed her off of him. I turned my back to him and prayed he didn't see me as I gulped the rest of my drink down.

Just a little less than two weeks ago he was warning me about him. Maybe about this. Trying to protect me from him. And I tried to cut off how I was feeling for him, but it's growing so naturally I swear it feels as if I have no control.

He's not my man. We're not committed to each other. Hell, I couldn't even kiss the man. None of that rationalizing the situation made me feel less hurt over seeing him with another woman.

Knight wrapped his right arm around me from behind and pulled me into his chest.

"You look beautiful," he whispered into my ear as his arm tightened around me.

"Knight…"

How could a kiss be soft and firm? That's how it felt when his lips branded my neck. It was soft enough to give me chills, but firm enough to make a river flow between my thighs. I grabbed his hand and tried to remove his arm, but he pushed me into the table softly and moaned as his dick pressed into me.

"I'm so happy to see you, Charlie."

"Charlie? Who the hell is this?"

That was Deja. All loud and possessive of me. I expected that to make Knight release me, but if anything, he held me tighter.

I met Deja's eyes and tried to focus on her, but the feel of his abs... his dick... his arm...

"Charlie..."

"This is Knight," I rushed out.

"Ohhh *this* is Knight," Deja smiled and placed the butt of her stick on the floor. Her hands went on top of it, and her chin rested on her hands. "I'd speak, but I don't think it would register at this point."

It wouldn't. He was too busy running his nose against my neck inhaling my scent to pay her or anyone else any attention.

"Knight, are you drunk?"

"No. I just miss you. I haven't seen you in like... three days, Charlie. If you don't want this kind of shit to happen I need to see you every day. As long as I can see you I don't have to feel you, but one or the other has to happen."

He kissed my neck again as he pulled me off the table and turned me to face him.

"My best friend is trying to speak to you."

Knight stared at me for a few seconds more before allowing his eyes to find Deja.

"What's up?"

"Hey."

"How are you?"

"I'm well."

Knight nodded and returned his eyes to me. His hand cupped my cheek and he caressed it with his thumb and pulled me closer at the same time.

"Why haven't I seen you?"

Why hadn't he seen me? I could say it was because I was busy with clients, but that wouldn't be the honest and complete truth. I was busy, but I wasn't too busy to see or talk to him. I just chose not to. Trying to stop these feelings that weren't listening.

"Who is that and why was she on your lap? Why is she looking over here like she wants to beat my ass?"

"Pah! She can try," Deja mumbled as she grabbed her drink off the pool table. "I'm going to the bar since your boyfriend has crashed our girl's night."

"He's not my boyfriend, and he'll be leaving soon."

"Why?" Knight asked.

"Because it's rude to leave your date alone to be talking to me."

"That girl ain't my date. I didn't even know she was going to be here."

"Who is she?"

Knight smiled and released me. He put some space between us and placed his hands in his pockets.

"A girl I used to mess with."

"You fuck her?"

"Charlie! I've never heard you curse before. That makes twice in less than five minutes."

"Did. You. Fuck. Her?"

"Yea. But that's all it was."

"Is that what you were going to do tonight?"

"No."

I didn't believe him, but it wasn't my place to question him anyway, so I nodded and tried to walk away. He grabbed my hand and pulled me back into him.

"I'm serious, Charlie. I'm not having sex with her or anyone else tonight."

"So you just let any and everybody sit on your lap?"

"You ain't sitting on it," I chuckled and shook my head as I looked at the ceiling. "Do you feel disrespected? Hurt? Angry? Did I do something wrong?"

"No. You didn't do anything at all. We're not together so it doesn't matter."

"Obviously it does. You can't look at me. Your body is stiff. Talk to me."

"There's nothing to talk about," I said as I clapped my hands together.

Was I clapping my hands right now? Was I really mad at him? Wow. Trying to find my center, I closed my eyes and pinched the bridge of my nose as I inhaled deeply. How could I allow him to have such control over my emotions? How could I go from feeling so happy and carefree to angry and possessive?

"Charlie, there's nothing going on between us. I haven't seen her in about six months. She thought she'd have a chance to start something up since I was home, but I told her that I wasn't interested. Yea, I let her sit on my lap and feel on me a little, to be honest the attention and affection felt good, but you have to believe me when I say I don't feel anything for her."

"Well apparently you don't feel anything for me either."

"No," he shook his head and took a step towards me.

His left hand was out of his pocket and he was pointing at me as he spoke.

"That's what we're not about to do. You're not about to tie this together. What I do with her or any other woman has nothing to do with how I feel about you. We agreed that we weren't going to let anything happen between us, but that doesn't mean I don't like you and care about you.

And just because I like you and care about you doesn't mean I'm not going to talk to other women.

If I don't, all of my attention will be on you. You'll be the only woman I give my energy and time to.

And if you're already feeling things for me you will *not* be able to handle me making you a priority. You *will* fall in love. Is that what you want? Right now, any woman can catch my sight and it not mean anything to me. Are you trying to be the only woman in my vision? Do you really want that to happen right now?"

"That's not a fair decision to ask me to make."

"Life ain't fair, beauty. If you don't want me socializing with other women, you need to start answering my phone calls and spending time with me. Is that what you want?"

"It's not that I don't..."

"But?"

"But I can't."

"Why?"

I grabbed the top of my shirt absently and squeezed.

"We agreed, Knight. No feelings. No relationship. Right?"

I couldn't give him things a normal woman could. I couldn't even kiss him. I couldn't be intimate with him. How could he have a future with me? Scarred, damaged, scary me? He was better off with her or anyone else at this point.

"If that's how you want to keep it, Charlie, fine. But your words and actions need to align with your desire. You can't get mad at me for shit like this when you aren't meeting my needs. You can't demand loyalty and fidelity when you aren't supplying the same plus love, attention, affection..."

"OK. Fine."

His pointing finger went under my chin, and he used it to lift my head. My eyes closed as I hoped this would be my second chance of getting this kissing thing right, but I realized that wouldn't be the case when I felt his lips at the side of my mouth. Soft. Smooth. Full. As pleasurable as I thought they'd be. He rested his forehead on mine as he hugged me.

My arms went around his neck at the same time I opened my eyes and looked into his.

He pulled me closer and the exchange happened. It was no longer our foreheads that were touching but our lips. The second they connected all parts of my body started reacting. My heart started pounding and skipping beats. Burning. My pussy throbbed. My stomach tightened. My arms covered with chills.

But just as quickly as he kissed me is just as quickly as he pulled away.

"Shit," he whispered as he let me go and stepped back. "I didn't mean to get that deep. I said I wasn't going to try to kiss you anymore."

"No it's... it's fine. I... I don't mind. Really."

"I'm sorry, Charlie. You and your friend be safe. Who's driving?"

"*What?*"

What the hell? Did he really just cut my kiss off like that and expect me to be coherent? Dude.

"Who's driving? Both of you are drinking..."

"I am. I only had one and that's all I'm going to have."

He nodded and took another step away from me.

"Cool. Text me and let me know when you've made it home safely, Charlie. That's not a option; it's a demand."

I closed my eyes and licked my lips – trying to taste the remnants of him.

"Charlie..."

"OK. I'll text you."

My eyes opened in time enough to see him looking me over from toe to head. His mouth opened, but instead of saying anything he walked out of the pool hall. Leaving me and the woman who was sitting on his lap standing dazed and confused.

Home

I sent the text to Knight then placed my phone on my bed. My mind was still spinning over the fact that I not only had an emotional reaction to seeing him with another woman, but that he put me in my place about it. Not only did he put me in my place about it but he kissed me. He kissed me. I haven't been kissed in years. And it felt so fucking good.

It felt good to be connected to another human being.

It sucked that he felt as if he had to hold back from me, but that's for the best. If I could barely handle the little peck he gave me, I can't imagine how I would have felt if he would've slipped me some tongue.

I'm all over the place. The first time he tried to kiss me I ran from it. Now I craved it. I guess as time passes and I spend more time with him the inevitable is happening – I'm falling for Knight Carver.

Hard.

As I pulled my shirt over my head I received a FaceTime request. I assumed it was Deja so I picked my phone up, but I was pleasantly surprised by the sight of Knight's name. I quickly put my shirt back on and accepted his request. Just the sight of him had me smiling as usual. He did the same and lowered his eyes briefly before looking at me.

"I just wanted to make sure we're good. I don't need you shutting down on Harlem because of me."

"We're fine, Knight. I told you I didn't mind the kiss. If anything I wanted more."

"I can come give you more. Right now."

There was something about the look in his eyes and the raspy sound of his voice that told me that wouldn't be all he'd be coming to give me, and I was reminded yet again of the fact that I would never have a normal relationship with him... or probably any other man. The thought made my heart literally ache. I felt my face twist as I clutched my chest.

"Charlie... what's wrong?"

"Nothing I'm just... tired. Headache."

Why did I lie? Why couldn't I tell him about my heart? About the scar? Why was I so afraid to share that part of me? That *was* me. Normally I was proud to say that I was a survivor, but with him... I was scared. Scared that it would end the façade he had of me, and that he'd lose interest and stop seeing me the way he did. And after years of feeling invisible my God I loved the way it felt to be seen.

"Well take some medicine and get some rest, beauty. We'll talk later."

"Will we?"

"If you want us to."

"I do."

"Then we will."

I felt like this was when I was supposed to end the conversation, but I couldn't. I just stared at him until he spoke again.

"Can I go to sleep looking at you tonight?"

"You mean in person or like this?"

He chuckled quietly and made me smile.

"Like this, Charlie."

"Sure," I said with my mouth, even though my mind screamed no. Pleaded with me to say no. "Let me shower and I'll call you back."

"Cool."

Knight disconnected the call and I just stood there for a second. Phone in hand. Trying to figure out how I was going to get through this night without falling for him even harder. When no solution came to me, I went through my drawers for something to sleep in. Normally I slept in my undies or naked, but since he was going to be looking at me I had to make sure my chest was covered completely. And that's when the tears started to pour.

How was the thing that was meant to give me life robbing me of it at the same time?

$\gtrsim$ **KNIGHT** $\lessgtr$

My baby sister was entering her fifth month of pregnancy with baby boy Hayden. For this doctor's appointment she warned me ahead of time that Tage was supposed to be here, and I gave her my word that I wouldn't cause any problems.

No matter how irritated I was by the fact that he was 15 minutes late, and when he walked in he nodded at her, sat next to her, and immediately buried his head in his phone. To avoid breaking my promise, I texted Charlie to get my mind off of things.

She and I had been talking a lot. Probably way more than we should have been talking. After she saw me with one of my old *friends* at Sticks and I damn near fondled her, well I guess I did fondle her, I was done hiding how I felt about her.

I liked her. A lot. And I didn't give a damn if she felt the same or not. If she wanted to feel the same or not. It had been years since any woman had captured my interest and held it, and I planned on taking full advantage of this. Of liking someone. Of wanting more from a woman than just random nights out and sex.

Fast or not.

Until I left... Charlie was mine.

I think she'd finally gotten the point because she stopped trying to deny the pull that was going on between us and started calling and texting me just as much as I was calling and texting her. We still only saw each other when she had to do something for Harlem, but that was practically every day anyway so it was cool.

How's your client? Is she still giving you a hard time?

I sent the text and put my phone on my lap. One of her new clients had a hard time admitting that she needed help. The only reason Charlie was there was because the woman's husband hired her. She didn't even want Charlie's help. In front of her husband she acted cool with Charlie's presence, but when he was gone she gave Charlie the hardest time.

Charlie said she'd give it to the end of the week to see if she'd lighten up. If not she was going to return the husband's money and quit.

I didn't blame her. The great thing about having your own business was that you chose who to do business with. All money ain't good money. I refuse to let anybody disrespect me just because they think the money they're paying me gives them the right to.

I was proud of Charlie, though. When I first met her I thought she was this soft, cheerful little thing that would never even hurt a fly, but the more I got to know her the more I learned she had a little G about herself.

Beauty: -_- She's got my Holy Spirit all out of whack. I'm trying SO hard. SOOOO hard.

"Who you texting? Better be Charlie since you over there smiling."

Harlem was leaning over the arm rest of my chair trying to look into my phone. I looked at her and smiled.

"Not that it's any of your business, but yes, I am texting Charlie."

"Umhm. Better be."

"Why do you like her so much anyway? You don't like anyone."

"I don't like the ones that aren't any good for you. She is."

"But how do you know that?"

Harlem shrugged and looked at the nurse as she opened the door.

"I don't know..."

"Harlem Carver."

We all stood as Harlem continued.

"Just something about her."

That was the same thing I'd said. I couldn't quite place what it was about Charlie... but it was just something about her. We went back to the room, and instead of me standing next to her like I did the last time, I sat in the seat that was behind her and allowed Tage to stand next to her.

It really didn't do any good.

The entire time her doctor talked to her and asked her questions he was in his phone or looking around the room.

Doctor James put that sticky shit on her stomach for the ultrasound, and before she could pull my boy up Harlem was looking up at Tage with that look. That look that I'd been waiting for her to have when it came to him.

"Tage, what's the point of you being here, bruh? Seriously."

"What you mean?"

"What do I mean? I mean you haven't said anything to me the whole time you've been here. You've shown no interest in asking Dr. James anything. And she's about to show you your baby and you're in your fucking phone."

I opened my mouth to check her about cursing, but I smiled and sat back in my seat fully prepared to enjoy the show.

"I'm here, Harlem. That's not enough? This ain't interesting to me. I don't think I'll be interested in none of this until he's actually here."

"You know what? You can leave."

"Har–"

"Goodbye, Tage."

I for sure thought he at least would have enough sense to try and fix his fuck up, but he didn't. He turned around and left. Just like that. Harlem looked back at me as she inhaled deeply and tried not to cry. She held her hand out for me and I immediately stood and made my way over to her.

"I'm proud of you," I told her before kissing her forehead.

"I'm proud of *you*. Thank you for not saying anything, Knight."

I nodded and turned my attention to the screen. His heartbeat filled the room and Harlem squeezed my hand as she smiled.

"Well, Harlem, there's your baby boy. Strong heartbeat. Let's see if we can get some movement while we have him on the monitor," Doctor James said.

Harlem's head shook and I looked down at her to make sure she was good.

"How could he not want to be a part of this, Knight?" she looked up at me with tears raining down her cheeks. "Every time I see him and hear his heartbeat it's even more real to me. How could he not want to be a part of this?"

Doctor James put the probe down and stood.

"I'm going to give you two some privacy."

Harlem's arms were wrapping around me as she cried harder, and it messed with my mental because this was the first time I'd seen her cry in years. Had me wanting to run out to the parking lot and beat his ass, but I held her and tried to comfort her as best as I could instead.

Food and shopping could always make Harlem feel better. We went to Osaka for food, then headed to the Wolfchase mall. About five stores in she was back to her normal happy self. On the ride there I questioned her to see where her head was at. She was cool, she just couldn't understand how he could be so detached from the situation.

I tried to get her to understand that she couldn't force him to feel the way she did or desire to want to be involved. Trying to do so would hurt her and the baby in the long run. You can't force a man to do or feel any type of way. If you want it to be genuine, you have to give him the space to get there on his own.

She said she understood and would give him the space to work everything out on his own, and I was hoping she meant that.

Harlem and I were headed to the movie theater inside of the mall when we spotted Charlie in the food court. She was all giggles and smiles with her arms wrapped around some dude's arm. All hugged up against the side of him. My feet were moving towards them before I even had a clue of what I was going to say or do, and Harlem was right behind me.

"Be nice about it," she said as she grabbed the back of my shirt to slow me down.

They sat down at a table and Charlie's back was to us, but whoever she was with saw us walking towards them. My face must have expressed the way I felt on the inside because his face hardened at the sight of it. Sensing the change in his mood, Charlie turned around to see what he was looking at.

She smiled even wider as she looked from me to Harlem. By the time we made it to their table she was on her feet with her arms open for Harlem.

"Hey, sweetheart. How was your appointment?"

Harlem hugged her and sighed. Charlie looked at me for an explanation, but I didn't give her one as I returned my attention to the man she had way too close to her body for my liking. Harlem released her and made her way back to my side, and I wasted no time sitting the bags down, grabbing Charlie, and pulling her into me for a hug.

She did this cute moan giggle before trying to remove herself from my chest, but I held on. I wanted it to be perfectly clear to ole boy that I didn't give a damn what they had going on – she was mine. Charlie kept her right arm around me as she said…

"Knight, this is my brother Rodney. Rodney, this is Knight and his sister Harlem."

Harlem waved as Rodney stood.

"Nice to meet you," Rodney said as he extended his hand for me.

I shook it and said the same. He shook Harlem's hand then sat back down. Feeling comfortable with letting her go, I released Charlie and she looked at me with a smirk before looking at Harlem.

"How did the appointment go?" she asked again.

"It was fine," Harlem answered finally as she slipped back into her sadness.

"Nope," Charlie lifted her chin. "Keep that head up. Don't let your crown fall. We'll talk."

Harlem nodded and hugged Charlie from the side. Charlie wrapped her arm around Harlem and pulled her away from us - completely ignoring me and her brother to tend to a visibly hurting Harlem.

"Have a seat," Rodney offered.

I waited until I couldn't see Harlem and Charlie anymore before I took Charlie's seat. This turned into some shit I wasn't prepared for today. I wasn't trying to meet the family and all of that.

"You looked at me like my sister was yours," he observed. "But she hasn't told me anything about you. How did you two meet?"

I had no problem answering his questions because I would've wanted to know the same if it was Harlem or Carmen, but if Charlie hadn't said anything about me to her family… maybe that was for a reason.

"If she hasn't said anything to you about me maybe she doesn't want you to know. I'd feel more comfortable with you having this conversation with her, but I will admit to this - I do like your sister. Very much. And I looked at her like she was mine because, well, she is. I might not be hers. We might not be in a committed relationship. But she is mine."

Seemingly pleased with my answer, Rodney crossed his arms over his chest and smiled.

"My sister is like fine china. Handle her well. If you break her, I'll kill you."

Now that got a good hearty laugh out of me. I hadn't been threatened by a big brother since I was in high school, but Charlie was worth it. This would be the first and only time he'd get away with this shit, though.

"Trust me, I have no intentions of hurting her. She's in good hands."

Hell, if anything, I was the one at risk of getting hurt. I had no problem at all taking things to the next level with Charlie, but she was holding back from me for whatever reason. It was like she was hiding something from me and whatever it was had guards up that I didn't even know how to climb over.

But then my nose caught her scent. And I looked to the right and saw her and Harlem walking over to us. And I saw the smile on her face. How it was like… the light of God captured in one place. And the desire to try and get her to open up to me and let me in grew even stronger.

Charlie

"Can you please tell me what room Evelyn Brown is in?" I asked the labor and delivery receptionist.

In the midst of shopping for dresses for the gala and auction, Evelyn, a third time around client, called to let me know that her water broke and she couldn't get in touch with her husband. At that moment, the fun that I was having with Rodney, Knight, and Harlem ceased and I had to go into servant mode.

I hadn't even planned on going to the mall with Rodney, but he called when I was on my way there and met me so we could spend some time together. When he found out what I was shopping for and realized he was in for an all-day thing he quickly tried to back out – didn't work!

I was kind of glad that he stayed since we ran into Knight and Harlem. He was the only person in my family that now knew about Knight, and I made no effort to try and deny the fact that I had feelings for him. It felt… good to express that to someone besides Deja. It felt… normal.

"She's in room 1094. Are you a member of the family?"

"No, I'm her… I don't know what you would call it…"

"Are you Charlie White? She told us to send you back as soon as you got here."

"Yes. I am."

"Perfect. Head around the desk to the left and take the second right. Her room is to the left."

"Great, thanks."

I rushed back to Evelyn's room, trying to get in touch with her husband for what felt like the millionth time, and yet again he didn't answer. If you ask me... he was having an affair. The three times I had to go up to his job when he was supposed to be there he wasn't. All of the calls to his cellphone were sent to his office during the day, and most men did the opposite. I felt like he was doing that to avoid having to talk to Evelyn, but whatever. That was none of my business.

The closer I got to her room the louder yelling and crying sounded off. It didn't sound like the type of yelling and crying that would come from a woman in labor. Especially a woman that was on her third baby. This sounded angry. I looked into the room before going in, and I saw Evelyn yelling at her husband, Adam.

Unsure of if I should go in or not, I placed my forehead on the door and listened to Evelyn's yelling.

"You come up here smelling like another woman when I'm having your child? You got the bitch's makeup on the collar of your shirt, Adam! Don't try to make me out to be the crazy one!"

"Mrs. Brown, please, try to calm down. Your blood pressure is elevating and we don't want to stress the baby," her doctor warned, and that was all I needed to hear.

I walked in, grabbed Adam, and walked right back out.

"Charlie..."

"Listen to me; get your shit together, Adam. Do *not* stress her out any more than she already is. What the hell were you thinking come up here like this?"

"I... I wasn't thinking, Charlie. I didn't want her to give birth without me being here. So I just left and came."

"But why were you even with another woman knowing your wife was going to go into labor at any moment?"

Adam leaned against the wall and hung his head.

"She was stressing me out, Charlie. Nagging me and complaining all the time. I just needed an escape."

"What did you just say?"

His head hung lower. With a roll of my eyes I went back into the room to Evelyn's side.

"Tell me what you need, Evelyn. Do you want him in here? In the waiting room? At home? What?" I asked as she grabbed my hand.

"I want him gone. He needs to go to my house, pack his shit, and make sure he's gone by the time I leave. You're going to stay here with me aren't you, Charlie?"

My smile was a bitter one as I ran my fingers through her hair.

"Don't I always? Let me go and get rid of him and I'll be right back."

She nodded and released my hand, and I made my way outside of her room to tell Adam her decision.

⇒ KNIGHT ⇐

This was the evening I'd been waiting for. Yea, the golf tournament was cool, and I enjoyed playing basketball, but this... the evening of the auction... this was what I was looking forward to most. This was probably the only chance I had to have a date with Charlie without having the pressure of dating and relationship expectations and all of that shit along with it.

I'd be able to take her out and enjoy her company one on one and not have to worry about things changing between us tomorrow morning – unless she wanted them to.

With that thought in mind, I was more than willing to pay any amount of money to possess her for the night.

"Well look at you," Harlem said through her smile as she made her way into my room. "Looking all fly and shit."

"Harlem..."

"I'm sorry. Stand over by the window so I can take a picture of you. You look so handsome, boo."

I looked myself over in the mirror once more. The Manhattan black & gold Brocade dinner jacket that I sported gave me a classic look. I paired it with a white button down and a pair of tailor-made black pants.

"Are you nervous?"

She would ask me that as she was about to take the picture. I wasn't necessarily nervous, but I was unsure of how she would react to me winning the auction and spending the night with me. I knew Charlie was nervous about the whole thing, and I wanted to make her as comfortable as I possibly could, but I was going to take full advantage of tonight.

"No. I'm not nervous. I'm just ready to get it over with. You make sure to text me and let me know when you've made it to Princess's house tonight. I might not text you right back, but I need to know that you've made it safely."

"Fine. Send me a picture of her when you see her. I know she's going to look beautiful."

I grabbed my keys and phone off the dresser and hugged Harlem before heading out. Yep, I was sure she was going to look beautiful too.

"Good evening everyone, and welcome to our first annual charity auction. Our new committee came up with a different and exciting auction for us tonight, and I hope you men have your checkbooks out and ready!"

Mrs. Berry, Doctor Berry's wife clapped her hands, encouraging the crowd to clap, as she paused. Her eyes went to the left of the stage and she nodded before she spoke again.

"Now, for those of you who filled out your cards to participate in the auction tonight, I'm going to give you a quick reminder of how this is going to work before we proceed."

OK. Maybe I was a *little* nervous. I slid down in my seat a little and released a quick breath as I ran my hand over my freshly chopped hair.

"Everyone will be bidding on one woman. All of your bids will be given to the hospital at the end of the night, but only the man with the highest bid will receive a date with our treasure when tonight's event is over."

Why was I nervous? She should want me to be the one to win. She knows me. We already spend time with each other, so it's not like I'm a total stranger.

"I called this young lady a treasure because that's exactly what she is. I've known her for a little over half of her life, and any man that wins a date with her will truly be getting a prize. A vessel of wealth. Not financially, but emotionally and mentally. This young lady is a jewel.

She has her own business. The heart of a servant. Her personality is warm and bubbly. Her smiles are bright and contagious. I just... can't say enough about her. So, without further ado, I present to you..."

This was it. This was it.

"Charlie White."

The sight of her not only affected me, but a great deal of men in the room. Their claps went from normal and light to fast and heavy as gasps and cheers filled the room. I found myself sitting up in my seat trying to get a better view of Charlie.

Her hair was flat ironed into a sleek, straight style with a part down the middle. Usually her makeup was natural if she wore any at all. Nothing special. She didn't need anything heavy or special. But tonight her face glowed. It glowed. And the deep burgundy lipstick that she had on kept pulling my attention to her lips.

That was... until I allowed my eyes to roam her body. The rose gold dress she had on complemented her beautiful brown skin perfectly. She looked beautiful. Classy. Elegant. Then she turned around and hugged Mrs. Berry and showed the backless design and added sexy to the list.

"Wow," came from on the side of me, and I couldn't have agreed more.

Charlie was beautiful.

Charlie was beauty.

The sequin gown accentuated her curves perfectly. All I could think about was pulling her into me by her hips and kissing her until all of her lipstick had been removed.

She blushed as applause and cheers continued all over the room, but I couldn't clap. I couldn't cheer. I couldn't do anything but take her in. When the room quieted down Mrs. Berry said...

"I refuse to start the bidding at anything less than twenty thousand."

That bid was quickly met and raised to 50. I wasn't expecting to be pissed at the bids being made for her. I mean... this was to be expected. But to have so many men wanting *my* woman? Mrs. Berry repeated a bid of a hundred thousand and regained my attention.

"150," I said as I raised my paddle.

This must have been the first time Charlie noticed me because her smile fell at the sight of me, then returned widely.

"Hi," she mouthed as she pulled her arms behind her.

I nodded and unbuttoned my jacket – fully prepared to go in for her fine ass.

"155," came from the opposite side of the room.

"175," came from behind me.

"200," I countered.

Charlie's eyes widened. Was she surprised that I had money or that the bidding was so high?

"250," came from the opposite side of the room.

"300," came from behind me.

"500," I countered.

Charlie took a step back as Mrs. Berry's mouth dropped.

"Is that a bid of five hundred thousand dollars?" she repeated. I nodded. "Five hundred going once..."

"505," came from the side of me.

"510," came from behind me.

I wasn't about to go back and forth with these folks all night.

"610," I countered.

"650," came from the side of me.

I looked over to see who it was for the first time, and he was already looking at me.

"700," I countered with a smile.

He scratched his nose and took a deep breath looking from me to Charlie.

"Seven hundred going once... seven hundred going twice..."

"725," came from the side of me.

I chuckled and stood. After buttoning my jacket back up I raised my paddle.

"One million."

Gasps. Whispers. Whistles. Cheers.

Charlie covered her mouth and took a few steps back.

"Wow. One million going once..." I stepped from behind my table and started making my way to the stage. "One million going twice..." the closer I got the more she backed away. "Sold to paddle number 13 for one million dollars!"

Hands were grabbing me as I made my way to her. I saw people on the sides of me clapping and cheering and talking to me... but none of that shit was registering. None of that meant anything to me. All I wanted to do was get to Charlie.

By the time I made it on stage she was backed into a corner with tears pouring from her eyes. Her mouth was still being covered by her hands. I pulled them down and kissed them both. Her eyes closed immediately.

"Knight," her voice trembled just as badly as her hands did. "Did you just... did you just spend a million dollars to go on a date with me? With *me*?"

Using my thumbs to wipe away her tears, I nodded.

"I had to have you. I had to claim you. I needed you to belong to me. To be mine. Even if it's just for one night."

"Knight... I..." her head shook before she lowered it and cried harder.

I took her hand into mine and led her backstage. When we were alone I pulled her into my arms and held her as she cried.

"Why are you crying, Charlie? Did you not want me to win?"

"I'm just surprised and happy and a little overwhelmed," she muttered as she sobbed.

That made me smile. And the fact that her arms wrapped tighter around me.

"Stop crying, beauty. I don't want your eyes red during our date. You've got two hours to get home and dressed. Get yourself together and text me your address."

I kissed her temple, dried her eyes one last time, then made my way back to Mrs. Berry to give her my check and head home to change clothes myself.

First of all; where did Knight even get a million dollars to bid on me? Seriously. Who bids on someone for a million dollars? Seriously. Like, OK. I know that he's a sports announcer, but sports announcers ain't making bank like *that*!

Second of all; who was I that he would even bid a million dollars on me? I expected some bids of a few thousand dollars for the charity, but the look in Knight's eyes was not one that burned for charity or the hospital. His eyes were trained on me.

Third of all; why did he have to look so good? That gold and black dinner jacket suited his style perfectly. The white shirt against his brown skin made him look edible. And the way his pants fit looked as if they were created especially for him.

And don't even get me started on his face and neatly trimmed hair and beard.

Good God.

Knight ruined me at that auction. Straight up ruined me. In a good way, though. One that I thoroughly enjoyed. One that would leave me tainted for the next man. No matter what happened between us after tonight, any man that tried to be with me from this point forward would have some big shoes to fill.

Who am I kidding?

Knight's shoes could *never* be filled.

My thoughts were all over the place when I made it home. Instead of getting dressed I spent about 45 minutes sitting at the edge of my bed thinking about Knight. It was obvious that we liked each other and were fighting it for our own hidden reasons, but tonight... there was no doubt in my mind that tonight would change everything between us.

Good or bad.

The ringing of my phone pulled me out of my thoughts. I wasn't expecting a call from Doctor Berry, so I immediately went into panic mode as I answered.

"Dr. Berry?"

"Hey, Charlie. Are you with Knight?"

"Not yet. Is something wrong?"

I stood and ran my hand across my stomach.

"Ah," he blew into the phone and I imagined him scratching his mustache as he used to do when he had to tell my parents something he didn't think they'd like to hear. "I'm not quite sure. I don't think there's anything wrong per se, I just... would like to speak with you soon. Can you stop by my office Monday?"

"Sure. Um... I can stop by before I start meeting with my clients. Around eight?"

"Perfect. I'll see you then. And thank you so much for participating in the auction tonight, Charlie. This one event brought in more than we've made so far all week."

"Oh no problem. No problem at all. I'm excited about the events for the rest of the week."

"Me too. Have a great night, Charlie."

"You as well."

I disconnected the call and made my way to my closet for something to wear. After choosing a strapless brown mermaid maxi dress I put my hair up and showered. The whole time I showered I questioned my choice of dress. It was linen, thin, and comfortable which is what I was going for, but it also was backless and tied at the top of my ass which could be a problem.

Knight had no problem expressing his attraction to me, and I didn't want to tease him. I didn't want to get him all hot and bothered and not be able to follow it up with sex. Was he expecting sex? Shit, I hope not.

After washing, I used my body scrub to make sure my skin would be soft, shiny, and smelling good just the way he liked. Any time I used the shea butter scrub I didn't have to use any lotion because it was so moisturizing, and that's the one I'd been using a lot since meeting Knight. The moment he made it clear that he liked the scent was the moment it became my every day choice.

By the time I was done reapplying my makeup Knight was ringing my doorbell. I quickly grabbed my robe and put it on as I made my way down the hall to let him in. Even though I knew it was him I looked in the peephole on my door to confirm.

I licked my lips and bit the top one as I unlocked the door. Standing behind it, I opened it wide enough to let him in. I closed it and grabbed the top of my robe... in no rush to turn around and face him.

"Sorry, I just need a few minutes," I informed him.

The feel of his hand around my wrist had me closing my eyes as he turned me to face him.

"You're worth the wait. I'm a little early anyway."

I opened my eyes and smiled at the bouquet of yellow roses in his hand. His hand dropped from my wrist, and he extended the opposite hand with the flowers inside.

"These are beautiful, Knight. Thank you so much."

He nodded as I took them and placed his hands in his pockets.

"I figured we could do dinner and whatever else you wanna do. I'm not really sure what you're into. Figured we could maybe get to know each other better tonight."

I took a natural step towards him and smiled when his nostrils flared as he inhaled my scent. Why was he holding back?

"That's fine, Knight. I'm down for whatever. Pool. Movie. Drinks. Hookah lounge. It's whatever."

His eyebrows lifted at the same time his mouth opened slightly.

"You're into that kind of shit?"

I chuckled a little and nodded as he took a step towards me.

"Absolutely. What did you think I was going to say?"

"I don't know, but I wasn't expecting that. I honestly thought you'd be a little uptight, but I can definitely rock with all of the suggestions you put out."

"Uptight? Really, Knight?"

"Yea, I mean, you haven't gone on a date in years and you've already expressed that tonight might be a bit uncomfortable for you. I figured you'd just want to come home after dinner."

My head shook as I closed the space between us.

"Knight, tonight you made the grandest gesture for me. You spent a million dollars to spend the night with me. Whatever I have to do to keep my nerves settled I will. I want tonight to be memorable for the both of us. Besides… this past month has given me the time needed to get comfortable with you. You're right, we don't know the facts about each other and all of that, but we vibe nicely. I don't think there's anything that could happen tonight that would make me uncomfortable."

His pointing finger slid across my collarbone gently as he licked his lips.

"In that case… hurry up and get dressed."

〜〜〜♥〜〜

We went to Flight for dinner, and as soon as we ordered our food and were alone I asked…

"OK, are you a drug dealer?"

He laughed, and I did too, but I was kind of serious. Those ebony eyes stared into mine until his laugh became a smile. Then he lowered them only to move his drink out of the way before looking at me again.

"I'm not a drug dealer, Charlie," Knight placed his hands on top of the table as he continued. "I used to play for the Grizzlies before I became an announcer. While playing I lived off of advertisements and put all of the money I made playing in the bank. When I retired I had about four years' worth of salary saved. So I'm living pretty comfortably right now."

"Really? I thought that you were really great during the basketball game, but it never entered my mind that you've played professionally before. Your life is so simple, Knight, I never would've guessed you were sitting on bank like that. I mean you have to have a lot of money to blow a million on this," I gestured at myself with one hand and the restaurant with the other. "But now that I think about it your house is pretty big, and your car is amazing."

That was true. I wanted to ask to drive his 2017 Lincoln MKZ as soon as I sat in the passenger seat, but I wasn't sure if he was one of those men who were super possessive of their cars so I bit my tongue.

"This," he pointed at me and the restaurant, "Is not something that I *blew* my money on. You were well worth the investment. If I would have had to go higher I would've, Charlie. Money to me is… just a resource for me to have the things I truly want in life. Spending a million or a billion to have a night with you?" he chuckled quietly and sat back in his seat with a shake of his head. "I'd do it again in a heartbeat."

"But I just don't understand why," I blurted with my frustration evident in my voice and face. "You could have any woman you want… why me?"

"If you think I'm a good enough man to have any woman I want... why wouldn't it be you? Who else would it be, beauty? There is no one else."

I finished my glass of Chardonnay and massaged my temples as he looked on and smiled.

"My attraction to you bothers you," he noticed. "Why?"

Our waiter walked by and noticed my glass was empty, so he offered to refill it, but Knight told him to bring us a bottle instead.

"It doesn't really bother me as much as it surprises me."

"Why would it surprise you? You're beautiful. Intelligent. Independent. One of the sweetest and most caring and loving people I've ever met. Why wouldn't I be attracted to you, Charlie?"

I shrugged and reached for my now full glass, but he pulled it away from me.

"I need you to open up, Charlie. I've given you more than enough time to not let me in. I need access tonight."

"OK. You first. Tell me about you. About your time in the NBA. Your past. Your family. I wanna know everything about you."

I could tell he felt some type of way about me deflecting, but he didn't object. Knight told me about his family. His mother and father. How his mother died when he was 22, and that she was the reason he left the NBA. How she asked him to finish college and get a degree before he went to the NBA but he didn't.

He went his first year of college and was hardly ever home because of it. His mother ended up getting sicker and sicker until death took her, and he felt so guilty about not being there for her that he stopped playing in the league.

"But you have to know that she wouldn't have wanted you to give up your dream for her, right?" I asked with watery eyes.

It broke my heart to watch him display his.

"I know that now, but 10 years ago I wasn't thinking rationally. I was hurting. I was angry. I was guilty. Still am. Just… it doesn't… consume me as much now."

"Have you ever considered going back to the NBA?"

"Honestly, no. I'm 32 years old, Charlie."

"So? Kobe retired when he was over 32, right? And I *know* Michael Jordan was old when he retired. I can't think of any other examples, but you're younger than both of them."

Knight smiled and stretched his arm across the table with his palm forward, and I placed my hand inside.

"This is really sweet of you, and it definitely makes me feel good, but… that time has passed for me."

"Oh, so, you think you wouldn't be able to hang anymore is what you're saying?"

"What? *Hell* no."

The disgust that covered his face made me laugh as he yanked his hand from mine.

"I'm just saying, Knight, if you think you can't hang…"

"I can hang."

"Then prove it," his face softened as he thought over my challenge. "You can practice with me." His smile returned.

"Practice with you? What you know about basketball?"

"I can play!"

"Mane, whatever."

"I can!"

"Ima make you prove that one day."

"Shit, we can play tonight."

"Charlie, don't play with me, girl."

"I'm serious. That can be what we do when we leave here."

Knight scratched his ear and nodded.

"Cool. I'm down. Now tell me about you. I've been wondering about that tattoo since I first saw it."

I ran my finger over the tattoo on my wrist. It was my first and only tattoo. The one that pretty much summed my life up to this point.

"It's three dates. My birthday, the day I was diagnosed with my heart condition, and the day I had my heart transplant."

"Wow. You had a heart transplant?"

His face softened as I smiled. This conversation was long overdue between the two of us. It was one of the... no it was *the* reason why I'd been so guarded with him. He deserved to know the truth, but I just... wasn't sure if this was the place to tell him *all* of it.

Our waiter brought our entrees out, but Knight pushed his food to the side as his eyes and attention remained on me.

"Yea, um... when I was born I had a heart murmur but it wasn't anything serious. I didn't start having trouble out of my heart until I was 13. I was on the majorette team at my school and I passed out during one of our performances. My parents took me to the hospital because even after I woke up and rested I was still tired and out of breath. My heart felt like it was about to beat out of my chest and I was so freaking scared.

It started with me having a problem with the left valve. Then it was the left and right. Then my heart started to enlarge. And by 19, 10 years ago, I needed a new one completely. I'd exhausted every other option at that point. The transplant was my last and only option, and even that wasn't guaranteed because my body could've rejected the heart.

But obviously it didn't," I smiled as a tear fell, but it wasn't a sad tear, it was a proud tear.

"So you're good now? I don't have to worry about you..."

He couldn't say it. He couldn't ask it.

"Dying?"

Knight nodded as his head lowered.

"Well, most transplant patients are given 10 years."

"10 years?" he repeated louder than I think he wanted to. "But that's... *now*. You could die now? Like any day now? What the fuck, Charlie?"

I giggled at the distressed look on his face as I reached for his hand. He gave it to me hesitantly. I'd come to grips with my fate. There was a chance that I'd live a full, normal life, and there was a chance that I wouldn't. The way I looked at it... people die young every day. I was just grateful for the extra time I was blessed with.

"There's a really good chance that I can live just as long as you. My heart is strong and healthy. I take my medicine daily. If I started to have any problems they would up my dosage or change my prescription and see what that would lead to, but I think I have a really good chance of living for a very long time."

He nodded, but he didn't seem reassured. And that's when I remembered what Harlem said about his fear of loss. How losing his mother made him not want to feel. Not want to love. Not want to lose. How he basically prepared himself to lose the people he cared about. I couldn't help but wonder if telling him about my heart transplant made him no longer want to pursue anything with me.

KNIGHT

10 years. She was told she had maybe 10 years to live, and now she's on year 10. Now that I've met her and started to fall deeply in love with her she's on year 10. She's on the year that could end her life and change mine in the process. Yea, there was a chance that she could live longer, but what were the odds of that happening? Really?

I was going to have to do some heavy research on this. There was no way in hell that I was going to fall in love with her only to lose her. No. I'd worked too hard to pull myself out of the hell losing my mother had put me in. I wasn't going to go back there. Not for love. Not when loving caused so much fucking pain.

The rest of dinner was quiet yet smooth. I didn't want her to think her telling me that had changed anything, but it kind of did. Still, I wanted tonight to be all that we both needed it to be, so when we made it to my home I tried to shake the sadness, worry, and fear that was consuming me off.

I wasn't even sure if us playing basketball was a good idea anymore.

I mean… what if she passed out or some shit?

I sighed louder than I wanted to as I cut my car off, and her hand reached over and grabbed mine.

"I'm OK, Knight. Please, don't treat me any differently. I shouldn't have even told you. I'm sorry for ruining tonight…"

"No," I kissed her hand and cursed myself for not hiding my emotions better, but dammit, I felt robbed before it even happened. "You didn't ruin anything. I'm glad you told me. I'm glad you told me, Charlie."

She turned her head and looked out of her window, and I knew I had to lighten this night up before she shut down on me again. I got out of the car and went to her side to let her out. We walked into my home hand in hand.

"Where's Harlem?" she asked as we went upstairs.

"Spending the rest of the week at her best friend's house."

"Oh. Um... your basketball court is in your bedroom?"

I looked at her and the hesitant look on her face made me smile.

"No. It's in the backyard. But you can't play in that dress."

Charlie looked down at herself and cursed under her breath.

"I forgot all about this. I need to go home and get something to wear."

"Why? You can put on one of my shirts and Harlem isn't that much smaller than you. I'm sure she has a pair of shorts you can put on."

She pulled her hand from mine and slowed her steps as we walked into my bedroom.

"Knight?"

After cutting the light on I looked at her.

"What's up?"

Her hands went through her hair as she swallowed hard.

"There's something else that I have to tell you. The reason why I haven't dated in years."

There was more?

Oh God.

I sat on the edge of my bed and ran my hand down my face.

"Go for it."

Her fingers intertwined in the center of her as she bit on her cheek.

"Well... I have a scar from my transplant," her eyes blinked rapidly as she pulled her hands apart. "It starts here," she pointed a few inches above her breasts. "And it ends here," she pointed a few inches under them. "When I was 20, I was about to give my virginity to this guy," she smiled as tears fell. "He was the first guy I ever felt comfortable enough with to show my body. My scar," her fingers ran down the center of her chest. Down the length of the scar. "But when he saw it..." her arms wrapped around her stomach. "His face... he looked at it... at *me*... like it was the most... disgusting thing he'd ever seen."

That explained all the button down shirts. All of the high neck dresses. She was insecure. She was ashamed of her scar. Her hands trembled as she used them to cover her face.

"I grabbed my clothes and ran. I haven't shown another man my body since. I haven't had the desire to. Until you," she pulled her hands down but avoided my eyes. "That's why I don't date. I don't kiss. I try not to get close to men. Because I know that eventually it's going to lead to sex and that's just something I can't do. I can't show another man my scar and have him look at me like that again. It would... I can't."

My head lowered as I put my elbows on my thighs. It all made sense now. I never would've guessed she'd be ashamed, but now that I think about how she reacted to me when I would touch her... when I tried to kiss her... how she'd pull at the top of her shirts when I looked her body over... it all made perfect sense.

"Come here, Charlie."

She took small steps towards me, and when she stood in front of me I grabbed her hands and looked up at her.

"That was not a man. That was a little boy. A little boy who didn't deserve you. A man," I turned her around and untied the back of her dress. "A man would worship that scar and the God who gave you a second chance at life."

"Knight..."

She grabbed my hand and tried to stop me, but nothing would stop me from correcting her fucked up way of thinking about herself. Her scar. Her story. Her blessing. I stood and took the thin straps of her dress between my fingers.

"A man would spend every day of his life thanking God for yours. Treating you like the blessing and miracle you are for gracing him with your life and presence."

I pushed the straps down, but it didn't fall to the ground. She grabbed it and clenched it in her fist. As I sat back down I turned her around to face me.

"Let it go, Charlie."

I didn't mean just the dress. I meant that memory. That pain. That shame. That insecurity.

"Knight," her head shook as her tears started to fall again. "Don't make me. I don't want it to change the way you see me. What you think about me."

"Let it go, Charlie."

Her eyebrows wrinkled as she chewed on her cheek again. She closed her eyes and dropped the dress. Her hands covered her face immediately as I took my time looking at the scar. At the thing that had her so afraid of men. Of me. Of love. Of sex. Of her body.

I opened my legs a little wider. Pulled her a little closer.

"*This* is what you've been hiding from me?" I ran my middle finger down her scar gently and she shivered under my touch. "You thought this would make you less beautiful in my eyes? This makes you even *more* beautiful to me. This makes you human. This makes you a survivor. This reminds me that I didn't just dream you up. This makes you *real*, Charlie."

I kissed the scar and her head flung back immediately. I worked my way up the scar, placing soft, slow kisses on every inch of it. By the time I was done she had a tight grip on my neck and shoulder as she panted.

Standing, I cupped her cheek and told her to look at me.

"You don't have to hide anything from me. I desire you just the way you are."

I brushed her tears away before placing both hands on her cheeks. The way she looked at me... it was different. It was like she was seeing me for the first time. Like I'd said what she'd needed to hear. What she'd longed to hear.

Her hands ran down my arms until they reached my wrists and she squeezed as her eyes closed and opened.

I cleared my throat and put some space between us.

"I'm gonna get the shirt so we can play."

Charlie grabbed my hand and pulled me back to her.

"Don't make me ask for it," she whispered. "Just give it to me."

"You're a virgin, Charlie. You should give that honor to... a man who deserves you. It should be a special moment, beauty."

"You *do* deserve me. I don't think I'll ever have a more special moment than this. Unless it came with you. Make love to me, Knight. Please."

Charlie

"You *do* deserve me. I don't think I'll ever have a more special moment than this. Unless it came with you. Make love to me, Knight. Please."

I meant that too. No man had ever made me feel the way he did. No man had ever talked to me the way he did. No man had ever soothed me the way he did. Made me feel strong in myself yet weak for him the way he did.

As if that was all the confirmation that I was ready that he needed, Knight pulled me into his chest and covered my lips with his. His pecks were just as soft the first time he kissed me, but this time there was an urgency there that wasn't previously.

His tongue slid into my mouth as he cupped my ass in both hands and pulled me closer. Giving me all of him to feel against me. I couldn't keep the moan that fell from my lips inside. Between the slow swirls of his tongue, his lips closing around mine and sucking them into his mouth, the feel of his dick against me, and his hands squeezing my ass… my pussy was throbbing at the same rate of my heart.

Knight pulled away from me only to grab and handful of my hair and tilt my head back.

"Are you sure?" he asked as he looked into my eyes intently. "I don't know how much teasing I can take."

"I'm positive."

"Undress me."

I exhaled a long, quiet breath as I unbuttoned his shirt. I focused attentively as I pulled his undershirt over his head. As if there was a certain way to do this and I wanted to get it just right. I needed to get it just right. I moved down to his pants, and he continued to look down at me with that same intense, inquisitive glare.

Knight stepped out of his shoes and pants. There was only one piece of clothing left. His boxers. I looked up at him... just to be sure if he wanted me to keep going. When he licked his lips and continued to stare down at me I put my thumbs inside of his boxers and pushed them down until they fell to his feet.

There it was.

"Touch it. It belongs to you now," he assured me.

I touched his head first. The crown first. And as soon as I did I felt his precum against my thumb. His dick jumped as he bit down on his lip. Lifting my hand, I looked at his cum on my thumb. It made me... curious. My thumb was in my mouth, and I was sucking the taste of him off of me before I think either of us was prepared for it.

Knight lifted me off my feet and tossed me over his shoulder as he carried me to his bed. His hands were pulling my panties down as soon as my body touched his bed. As in a rush as he was to get me in his bed, when he removed my panties and spread my legs his movement stopped. He stared at my pussy until it throbbed in desire for him.

"I'm glad you've kept yourself hidden," he confessed as he crawled deeper between my legs and hovered over me. "Now I'll be the only man to show you how beautiful and rare and sexy you are."

His fingers went into my hair as I smiled and ran mine across his scruffy beard.

"How long can I adore you, Charlie?"

My answer was locked inside of my brain at the feel of his dick between my legs and tongue on my neck. I grabbed his waist and squeezed as his teeth bit down on me.

"How long?"

"For as long as you want, Knight."

"Forever?"

"Forever."

His lips were on mine again. Sucking. Tongue. Licking. Teeth. Biting. Me. Moaning. The trail his mouth took sent shivers through my body. I watched as he kissed and licked his way down my breasts. My chest. My scar. My stomach. Until he landed between my thighs. No man had ever made it this far before, and the smile on Knight's face made it clear that he was glad about that as his palms gripped my thighs and spread them widely.

Knight placed a kiss to my left thigh before running his lips and cheek over the place he kissed, causing my back to arch off the bed from the feel of his facial hair tickling me. He did the same to the right thigh and got the same reaction.

"This is your last chance to back out," he warned me, only to run his tongue from my ass to the tip of my clit.

Loving the surge of pleasure that welled up within me, I instructed him to, "Do that some more."

He smiled, which made me smile, but when he ran his tongue between my bottom set of lips my smile faded as I inhaled deeply. At first his licking was slow. Soft. Precise. As if he was giving me time to get used to what he was doing to me. He'd suck my clit into his mouth after every few licks, but pull away when my legs would start to tremble and close against him.

Then I felt my clit harden. And I saw him stick his tongue inside of me and pull my nectar out. And all of the reserve I had was gone. My hands went to his shoulders and I squeezed as I moaned and gave myself to how good he was making me feel.

His tongue was harder. His licks were faster. Fuller. His slurping was louder. His sucking was harder. It lasted longer. He stuck his tongue inside of me deeper. He pulled my clit and my pussy lips into his mouth and sucked and licked at the same time until my legs trembled. Until the walls of my pussy throbbed. Until I pushed him away and cried out. Until I came for the first time in my life.

And he watched. *We* watched. As my nectar slid out me and made its way down my pussy as it throbbed. Knight moaned as he lowered himself to lick every drop of me up, not leaving anything behind.

Knight stood and walked over to his nightstand. He grabbed a condom and ripped it open as he watched me watch him.

"I don't have anything, but this is for your protection. I'm not trying to get you pregnant, and I know I'm not going to want to pull out."

I nodded and grabbed a handful of my hair as my legs opened and closed. I didn't care about any of that right now. All I cared about was having him inside of me. I'm glad he thought enough about it for the both of us, though.

Knight rolled the condom onto himself, and my anticipation was slowly being replaced with anxiety as I watched it... as I watched him... come back to me. Nothing had been inside of me but my fingers and tampons... and he expected me to fit all of *that* inside? He was long. And wide. And curved. And veiny. And everything. And the sight of it standing straight up as he crawled between my legs again had me swallowing hard and inhaling deeply.

He secured my legs around his waist and pushed my hair out of my face, and the way he looked down on me with such care and gentleness... it removed any anxiety I had.

"If you want me to stop at any time say so. It's going to hurt at first, but I promise I'm going to make you feel good. You just have to relax, Charlie. Do not tense up and fight it. I need this pussy to stay wet for me."

I nodded and pulled his face down to mine – trying to use kissing him as a distraction. It worked for a little while. It worked as he began to slowly press his way inside of me. By the time he had just his crown in I was biting down on his lip and moaning.

"That's right, beauty. Bite me. Scratch me. Do whatever you gotta do. But don't tense up."

He wrapped my arms around his neck and continued to inch himself inside of me slowly, only to pull himself out completely when he was halfway in. I started to ask him what the hell he was doing, but the wetness that had covered him from inside of me made it so much easier for him to slide in the second time around. This time he didn't go in inch by inch. This time he pressed himself inside of me until all of him was inside.

I moaned and pulled him closer, wrapped my legs around him tighter, but it was over. He was in. All of him.

"Are you OK?" he asked breathlessly.

I nodded, afraid that if I spoke my voice would say the opposite. He pulled himself out, heating my body with the friction of our disconnect. He pushed himself in, burying himself as deep inside of me as he could go. Our lips locked as he rocked his hips against mine, but it started to feel so good I had to pull away.

Moans were erupting from within me so consistently I had no control over them. I was cursing. And touching and scratching and squeezing his body in any place I could grab. And my stomach was tightening. My pussy was holding onto him. Tightly. Taking his slow, deep strokes and giving him wetness in return. Squeezing him and smacking against him and throbbing as I came. As my legs trembled and unraveled against him.

Knight secured the back of my knees in the bend of his arms and spread my legs as wide as they would go. His body rested against mine as he sank into me deeply. With his mouth next to my ear he asked...

"Can I fuck you now?"

I didn't think I could get wetter. Get more turned on. But he proved me wrong. I ran my hands down the back of his head and placed them around his neck as I nodded.

"Yes."

I wasn't prepared to feel him even deeper, but that's exactly what happened in this position. Each stroke felt longer. Deeper. It was faster. Harder. His pelvis was brushing against my clit, making every stroke feel magnified. Making every moan turn into curses that were abruptly cut off along with my breath. Making me grow completely silent before crying out his name. Making me stop breathing. Making me not care about not breathing. Making me breathe *him*. Making me try to push him away, yet pull him deeper into me by his thighs.

I was gone. Lost. Out of my fucking mind. Completely under his spell in this moment at the same time.

And then his heavy breathing turned into moaning and that turned into my name and I came again. So did he. Stopping his strokes while his dick throbbed inside of me. He moaned one last long time as he pulled my hair and shriveled up inside of me.

My arms and legs wrapped around him, and I held on... like I'd die if I let go.

"You can't leave me, Charlie."

Knight lifted his head and looked into my eyes. My hand immediately went to his cheek and I caressed it with my thumb. I had to live. Even if it was just for him. Even if it was just to avoid him having to take another loss.

"I won't."

"Promise me," he shook his head and lowered it. "That doesn't really mean anything. Shit happens. But it would damn sure make me feel at ease to hear you say it."

A small smile lifted my mouth as I raised up slightly and kissed him.

"I promise, Knight. I'm not leaving you."

He removed himself from inside of me and sat on the edge of his bed. I found myself wanting to still be attached to him in some way, so I rubbed his back until he stood and went into his bathroom. He came out after starting the water in his tub and discarding of the condom, then went out of his bedroom. When he returned it was with a bottle of bubble bath.

"Don't tell Harlem I used any of this."

I sat up in the bed and smiled as I shook my head.

He came for me.

Knight lifted me out of the bed and carried me into his bathroom.

"You need to soak so you won't be too sore. Now that I've had you I need you regularly."

"How regularly?" I asked as he placed me inside of the water.

"Daily. At least once a day. I'd prefer to have you to start and end my day."

Knight leaned against the wall, giving me the perfect view of his smooth chestnut skin.

"Get in with me."

He wasted no time getting behind me and pulling me into his chest.

"Charlie?"

"Yes?"

"Are we still playing basketball tonight?"

⋟ KNIGHT ⋞

We spent half the night playing basketball. Charlie wasn't bad at all. Not bad at all. Surprised the hell out of me honestly. I wasn't expecting her to have any real talent at it. I thought she was going to spend most of her time trying to distract me and grab up on me like most women did when they tried to play with me, but she actually had a little game. That only made me like her even more.

Around four this morning we finally called it a night. We showered together and crashed. Charlie woke me up with breakfast in bed, then I put her back to sleep with this dick. I convinced her to spend the rest of the week with me, so I dropped her off to freshen up and pack a bag while I stopped by my pops house.

Charlie and I were in a damn good space today, but everything that she shared with me last night had been replaying in my mind. She was a virgin. She gave me her virginity. She gave me the essence of her womanhood. That made me want to keep her even more.

As sweet and loving as she is, to know that a man had scarred in a way that could have been more permanent than her physical scar really fucked with me. I couldn't understand how anyone could want to do anything but love and take care of Charlie's ass, but I was kind of glad that he did hurt her. Hurting her made her shut down and remain perfectly preserved for me. And you better believe I planned on showering her with all of the love she could stand from this point forward.

Even with that desire, I couldn't shake the fear of losing her. Of her dying on me. *With* me. I planned on doing some serious research on heart transplants. I needed to actually see or even meet someone that was living well over their 10 year estimated life span. Until I was able to do that, I did what I knew how to do best – prepare for loss.

That's what led me to stopping by my father's house. Yea, he was back to being my pops too. We hadn't spoken since I asked about Harlem, but now I needed advice and he was the perfect person to give it to me.

I knocked instead of using my key again. As far as I was concerned, this was no longer my home. It stopped being that when my mama died. He opened the door and sighed deeply when he saw me. Like he knew I was about to be on some shit.

"I didn't come here to cause any trouble," I let him know quickly. He nodded and leaned against the doorframe – crossing his arms and ankles. "Did you love my mother?"

He chuckled and shook his head as he looked towards the sky.

"Of course I loved your mother. Loved her so much losing her destroyed me. I loved her too much. Couldn't even function after she was gone."

"I don't want to be like you. When I... if I ever lost the woman I love with all of me... I don't want to handle it like you. Tell me what I need to do to not be like you."

His head dropped as he ran his hand over the top of it. He stepped to the side and opened the door wider.

"Come in, son."

I walked into the home I grew up in, the home I learned how to love and hate in, and this overwhelming heaviness covered me. It wasn't until I was faced with losing Charlie, a woman I had just met, that I began to understand my father's position. That I began to have my mind opened to how losing my mother could've changed him. And even with that realization, I still understood that I wouldn't be able to even remotely understand how it felt to lose the woman you saw forever with.

The woman you spent 30 years with. Had kids with. Built a life with. Only to have to see her face in her children every day.

I felt guilt, but not the guilt that I'd been feeling over the years because of not being here for my mother. I felt guilty about how I'd been treating my father. I fell to my knees before him and begged for his forgiveness – knowing when I got up I'd be stronger. Wiser. A better man. Knowing that besides God and my future wife, he'd be the only man I'd ever bow to.

His arms wrapped around me as he kissed the top of my head.

"It's OK," he assured me as he lifted me to my feet. "I knew this day would come. It's OK."

We hugged. Hard. And I cried. For him. For my mother. For my sisters. For Charlie. Cried for her before I even lost her because I wasn't sure I'd be able to if I did. After I gathered myself and he did the same we walked into the living room and sat down.

"You met a woman," he said more than asked.

"What makes you say that?"

"That's the only thing that would make you come here and feel my pain the way you did. Love is the only thing that makes you feel that kind of pain."

I smiled as I sat back in my seat and thought of Charlie. I met more than just a woman. I met my heart. And I'd be willing to give her mine so she could stay here and raise our kids if the time and need ever arose.

"Yea. I met a woman."

"You plan on marrying her?"

"It's still early. We're not even committed to each other."

"You plan on marrying her?"

Who was I kidding? I knew the minute I laid eyes on Charlie that I wanted her. And I knew within seconds of talking to her that she'd be mine. And when she revealed herself to me I knew she was the one.

"Yea. If she'll have me."

"Don't take her for granted," his eyes shifted to the picture of him and my mother hanging on the wall. "Value every day that you have her and make sure that she knows via your words and actions just how much you love and cherish her. Don't take advantage of her. Be loyal and faithful. Be the man I raised you to be. Provide for her. Protect her. Give your life for your family if necessary.

Cultivate her and make her better. If she should leave this world before you do..." he inhaled deeply as his jaw clenched. His head hung briefly as he licked his lips. "Understand that she would want what was best for you and your family with her. She'd want you to let her go. She'd want you to live for the both of you. Not in anger. Not in guilt. Not in pain. But in love."

His head shook as he looked inside of his empty hands.

"You can't love her with all of your heart. You've got to love her with your soul. Love her with your spirit. Your heart is the seat of your emotions. Emotions... feelings... they change. They waver. They're inconsistent. Your soul is how you connect with humans. It's your morality. It's who you are. At the very core of your being.

Your spirit is how you connect with God. Love her with your soul by connecting with her mentally. By being the man she needs to lead her. Love her with your spirit by growing closer to God and leading her to him.

Above all... keep in mind every day of your life that every day of your life is not guaranteed. Every day is a gift. A present. Make the most out of every day that you have with her. Don't worry about losing her. Don't worry about materialistic things or things that don't matter. Things that hold no true weight in your life. Make memories.

Make memories. Don't exist and allow life to pass either of you by. Live. Explore all that life has to offer you together so that when the day comes... because it will come... and one of you leaves... the other will have enough memories to hold them over until you meet again."

He stood and went somewhere, giving me a lot to think over in his absence. When he returned he handed me the box that held my mother's wedding ring.

"Don't allow fear to rob you of her. Don't waste time. When you get to the point of not being able to live without her... don't."

Charlie

Knight and I made love. We fucked. He kissed my scar. Ran his fingers up and down it every chance he got. Kissed me every chance he got.

Knight and I made love.

After waiting 29 years I gave myself to a man. Finally. And I don't regret it at all.

When it was time for me to leave this morning he asked me to stay for the rest of the week and I wasted no time agreeing! I had no idea what he had planned for us, but I would've been fine just sitting in the middle of his bed staring at him and letting him stare at me.

On my way back to his place I had to stop by a client's house for a pamper session – mani and pedi along with a slight massage. I loved the pamper sessions because they relaxed the moms and gave them time to focus on themselves for a change.

As I grabbed my kit I received a call from Harlem. Since it was the middle of the day and her ass was supposed to be in class I started to worry immediately. I dropped the kit back on the backseat and answered her call.

"Hey, sweetheart. What's wrong?"

"Hey, Charlie. Nothing. What you doing?"

Leaning against my car, I looked at the phone and smiled.

"Harlem, aren't you at school?"

"Yea, but I'm on lunch. Um… I was calling to see what the name of that show was that you mentioned? I wanna watch it with Princess when we get out of school."

She had to either be talking about Longmire or Sneaky Pete. I remembered telling her about how I hadn't had hardly any time to watch any of my favorite shows when we first met and I was still working at Bundle. The day we started putting the baby's stuff up we ended up watching SpongeBob and Alvin and the Chipmunks the entire time.

Those are two of my favorites too. They're relaxing and funny. Don't judge me.

"You mean Longmire or Sneaky Pete?"

"Yea, yea. Those. Which one did we watch that one episode of last week when you stopped by the house?"

"That was Longmire."

"OK cool. Soooo how was the auction? I told Knight to send me a picture of you but he forgot."

Just at the mentioning of last night and his name I started pining for him. I squeezed my legs together as I pulled at my hair – wishing his hand was in the place of mine.

"It was so much fun, Harlem. So much fun. I'll send you a couple of pictures when we get off the phone."

"Knight won the auction, right? I know he did. I know my boo came through."

"He told you about that?"

"Yep. He was nervous as hell. Talking about he refused to let another man claim you. I helped him find something to wear."

I grabbed my kit and used my hip to close the door with a smile.

"Well, you did a great job because he looked amazing last night, and yes… he won."

Not just the auction but me. My eyes. My attention. My body. My heart. My soul. My all. Not because of the money. It wasn't like the million was coming to me. But because of what that million represented. It forced me to see him. See his desire for me. There was no way I could ignore how either of us felt from that point forward.

"Yaaaassss I have to call him and get all the details! I'll talk to you later, sis."

She abruptly ended the call before I could even say goodbye. I was laughing so hard at her thinking Knight was going to share the details of last night with her that I didn't realize she'd call me sis until I was at Mya's door putting my phone up to ring the doorbell.

Listen, I couldn't have made it back to Knight any faster no matter how hard I tried. It felt like... there was no other place I'd rather be than with him. That was all I could think about when I was with Mya. Getting back to Knight. I rushed back to his place as quickly as I could.

It wasn't until I got there that I figured I should ask if he was hungry. I called him as soon as I pulled into his driveway and asked if he had anything in there for me to cook. He told me that wouldn't be necessary as he opened his front door and came outside.

I heard the phone beep from him disconnecting the call, but I still held it to my ear as I watched him. He licked his lips and put his phone in the pocket of his shorts with his right hand as he ran his left hand over the top of his head.

I know this is going to sound so corny, but as he walked towards my car it was like everything around us faded away. Like his movements were in slow motion. His eyebrows lifted as he locked eyes with me and smiled, and I was still just sitting there in the car with my phone to my ear.

Knight opened my door with a chuckle. He took my phone and put it in the same pocket he put his in, then grabbed my hand and pulled me out of the car. His hands cupped my cheeks and he used them to pull me into his chest. Onto his lips. I gripped the sides of his shirt as our tongues connected.

My nipples hardened instantly as he swirled his tongue around mine slowly. The thought of how it felt against my clit last night and this morning had my pussy throbbing as I bit down on my lip. His hand moved from my cheek to my jaw. Knight squeezed until I released my bottom lip and returned to kissing his.

With no care or concern to being outside in the middle of the day, I tossed my arms around his neck and pulled us to my car to get more comfortable.

He groaned and lowered his hands – allowing them to roam my body freely. They were in my hair. Around my neck. Squeezing my breasts. Gripping my thighs. Lifting my thighs. Wrapping them around his waist. Cupping my pussy. But when he did that and brushed my scar my back arched against him as my entire body shuddered.

I wiggled until I was back on the ground with space between us.

"You are *not* about to make me cum in front of your neighbors," I reprimanded breathlessly as I ran my fingers through my hair and pulled it out of my face.

"I missed you."

Knight grabbed my shirt and returned me to his chest.

"I missed you too. I couldn't wait to finish with my client so I could get back here to you."

"That sounds good, Charlie. Getting back here to me."

I smiled and turned to grab my bag out of the backseat, but he stopped me and got it himself.

"Thank you."

I got my purse and locked my car before following him into his home.

"Ima take your bag up to my room. You wanna change into something more comfortable?"

I looked down at the button down shirt I had on and up at him. His shirt would've been the most comfortable thing I could've worn. Knight made me bold. He made me feel sexy. He made me confident. He made me feel comfortable in my own skin. I smiled and lowered my head as I started to unbutton my shirt and follow him into his room.

He walked in first, and when I walked in and saw that his bed was covered with pizza and snacks I gasped. Longmire was paused on his TV. Why was I about to cry? Why was I as emotional about something so simple and thoughtful as I was for something so extreme and grand like what he did at the auction? My hands went from the last button on my shirt to my face and I covered it to hide the tears that threatened to fall.

This was why Harlem called me. For him.

Knight undid the last button on my shirt and pulled it down. I had to drop my hands in order for him to get the shirt off completely, so I inhaled deeply and let my hands down. The second I did our eyes locked. He continued to remove my shirt and bra as his eyes remained on mine.

"I wanted you to be surprised so I had Harlem to call and ask. Figured we could just chill today since you didn't have much to do for your clients. Unless you wanna go out tonight…"

My chest smacked into his as I hugged him tightly. Unsatisfied with our lack of closeness, I continued to push myself into him… just… trying to get closer. Knight chuckled as he wrapped my legs around him and held me just as tight. He kissed my neck and let out a soft sigh.

"You smell so good, Charlie. I hope you brought whatever the hell this scent is with you."

"Knight…" I lifted my head from his shoulder and looked from his eyes to his lips as I caressed his scruffy beard. "You can't *do* stuff like this."

I inhaled deeply as my lips trembled. Fighting terribly hard not to cry. Not to be *that* girl. The one who hadn't had this kind of love and care from a man besides family, so she didn't know how to act when she got it.

"Why not?"

He lifted my head with his finger under my chin. I hadn't even realized I'd lowered it.

"It's gonna make me fall in love with you."

"You don't want to? I wanna fall in love with you."

"You do?"

"I do. I *am* falling in love with you."

"You are?"

"I am."

"Oh. OK. That's perfect cause… I'm falling in love with you too."

He smiled but it didn't last long. It was replaced with him licking his lips and placing me against the wall. Longmire could wait for just a little while longer. I needed him inside of me… and the way he tugged at my jeans let me know he wanted to be inside of me just as badly.

⇒ KNIGHT ⇐

By the time we'd finished watching the fifth season of Longmire and first of Sneaky Pete it was well into the next morning, but neither of us was in a rush to go to sleep. For me, we'd spent so much time running away from each other that now that I had her I didn't want to waste any time. Not even sleeping. Either she felt the same way or was used to staying up late and was just going with the flow.

We'd cleared the snacks off the bed by now and were just... talking. Charlie was sitting at the top of the bed and I was laying across the middle. I wanted to get to know her better. I wanted to know everything about her. What made her happy. What pissed her off. What turned her on.

I wanted to be able to control her emotions at all times. I wanted her to want me just as much as I wanted her. I wanted us to be so connected and in tune with each other that another man complimenting her and trying to snatch her from me would be an insult to her.

She'd just finished telling me about her goals. How she wanted to get a storefront for her business and link up with a few baby supplies wholesalers to stock her store. She wanted to up her clientele from 10 clients per season as she called it to 20. How she wanted to hire an assistant, preferably somebody named Brea, so she would be able to enjoy the fruits of her labor more.

Then she asked me what my goals were. I hadn't shared them with anyone before, so it was a little awkward for me to start, but when I did it was natural.

"I want to start some kind of program for kids. Where basketball and business are connected. Something that they can do from the start of high school to graduation that will guarantee them an academic scholarship if they complete the program. I also want to go into..."

Charlie smiled widely as she pulled her knees to her chest and wrapped her arms around them. She placed her chin on top of her knees and stared at me with such interest and attention that I just... completely lost my train of thought.

"What's wrong, Knight?"

Her smile fell and I shook my head as I relaxed my face and tried to pull myself out of her spell.

"Nothing. I just... you looking at me like that... listening to me... made me forget everything I had to say."

Her smile returned as she crawled over to me, making my dick grow with each inch of space that she removed from us. Charlie made herself comfortable on my lap. Running her hand down the back of my head as she stared into my eyes.

"You never had a woman listen to you before?"

"I guess not. Not in a way that made me feel like they were actually interested or genuinely cared about what I had to say."

She kissed my lips softly. And slow. Giving them enough time to linger there and leave how she felt behind.

"Well I am interested. I do care. I am listening. So continue."

I couldn't right away. I kissed her chin and her lips through her smile. Then the side of her mouth.

"What was I saying, beauty?"

"Scholarship program. You also want to go into?"

"Right. Right. Coaching."

"On what level?"

"Definitely not the NBA. Not anymore. Before Harlem got pregnant..." and before I met her... "I wanted to coach in the NBA, but it just takes up too much time. I would never be home. Even during the off season I'd have to be with the team helping them train. I'd have to be on the road scouting new players. The only reason I'm completely free now is with announcing I only have to be with them for the off season games, and those won't be happening for a little while.

I'm not sure how things are going to turn out with her and Page..."

"Tage, Knight."

"With him, and I just wanna be here for her. With that being said, college or grade school would be cool. High school might be perfect. Especially if I get my program up and running. Maybe put something together with mid-south high schools and colleges where the players can take a couple of business courses while in high school that will count as credits when they start college. Keep them from being in the position I was in when I was in school."

"And what position was that?"

"Having to choose between staying in school and finishing my degree or dropping out and living my dream."

"You regret the choice you made?"

"Not because I missed out on my degree. I have more than enough money and it's working for me because I know how to invest and flip it. But I do regret it because had I stayed in school I would've been home and graduated like my mom wanted me to."

I didn't want to go into that depressing shit, so I cut her off the second her eyes saddened.

"I don't want to go there, Charlie. Not right now. I feel too good with you right now to go there."

She nodded and rested her forehead on mine.

"Do you think she would've liked me?"

Her hands went from the back of my head to my cheeks. I pulled her closer and rubbed her pussy against my dick in the process. The feel of her wetness and heat had me losing my train of thought again.

"Knight..."

"Yea, babe?"

"I said do you think she would've liked me?"

"She would've loved you, Charlie," we sat in silence for a while before I asked her, "If you had the time and money to do anything in this world what would it be?"

"Travel. A lot," she smiled and went off into her own little world. "I want to be able to travel a minimum of once a month every month by next year. The goal is to eventually have a team working for me so I won't have to work unless I want to. Then all of my time will be freed up to explore other sides of life. Like traveling and..." her eyes returned to mine. "I wanna get married and have curly haired babies. Do you wanna get married, Knight?"

"In general or to you?"

Her head lowered as she tried to hide her smile.

"In general."

"Don't be a punk, Charlie."

"Knight!"

She tried to remove herself from my lap, but I held on to her waist.

"You don't give a damn if I want to be married in general. Your only concern is if I want to be married to you. Right?"

And she had every right to want to know that. I didn't believe in wasting a woman's time. Leading her on and making her believe she had more of a chance with me than she actually did. It wasn't until now that I realized Charlie and I didn't even have a title between us.

I guess when you know how you really feel about someone and what you want to give them and get from them... none of that other shit really matters. Still, as a woman she needed to actually hear me say how I felt. What I planned on showing her through my actions.

Her eyes returned to mine along with that smile that I swear I couldn't get enough of.

"Right."

"I do. I wanna marry you," her chest inflated as she took in a deep breath. "Haven't given it much thought, but I've known for quite some time that this whole you walking out of my life after Hayden is born thing was bullshit. I wasn't sure how I was going to keep you forever, but I knew immediately that you were the kind of woman that needed to be kept. But only by me."

Her eyebrows wrinkled in frustration as she chewed on her cheek. I thought she was about to say she wasn't ready to hear that yet. That she didn't feel the same. That I was in this alone. But what she did say shattered what little guards I had left up.

"Make me what you want, Knight. Make me what you need."

"*Charlie...* you already are."

She closed her eyes and inhaled deeply, and I took advantage of that moment. I kissed her and held her as she melted into me. Her arms wrapped around my neck as mine went around her waist. Small, delicate fingers ran down the back of my head. Soft sighs of pleasure fell from her lips. This girl was going to be the death of me and she had no fucking clue the kind of power she had over me.

I pulled away, only to stand and walk over to my nightstand. No matter how much I wanted to feel her walls in their most vulnerable state, I would always wear a condom. She had a plan for her life and I would not be the fuck boy that ruined it by getting her pregnant. Even if I did plan on marrying her and being there with her and our seed every step of the way.

We were going to do this the right way. Her way. With us falling completely in love with each other. Enjoying each other selfishly. Getting to know each other as friends, lovers, spouses... and then as parents.

I sat on the edge of the bed and pulled my shirt over her head. For some reason I was fascinated with her scar. The thing she was ashamed of most... I cherished most. I found it to be the most beautiful part of her. Maybe because deep down in the back of my heart or mind or both I knew she needed me to. And I wanted to give her all that she wanted and needed.

It was either going to be ripping her panties off or pushing them to the side. Allowing her to get up and take them off wasn't an option at this point. I couldn't take my lap not having her there anymore.

Charlie lifted my shirt over my head before returning her lips to mine. I opened the condom and slid it on as quickly yet carefully as I could.

"Is it wet for me?" I asked against her lips.

I didn't mind foreplay. In fact, I *loved* foreplay. I understood the more I pleased a woman the wetter she'd be. The more she'd accept me. The more pleasurable it would be for me. But right now, I just needed to be in her. In my woman.

"Always."

That alone had me close to exploding, but I would never get mine before giving her hers. I gripped her hips and lifted her enough to slide her back down onto me. She made her way down carefully. As if she was fighting it just as hard as I was. And by the time her tightness and wetness had molded against me I was cursing under my breath and keeping her still.

Like I hadn't had her when she first got here.

Like I hadn't had her twice the day before.

Like I couldn't get enough of her.

I couldn't.

Her inexperience didn't take away from the fact that her pussy was the best I'd ever had. Yea, I'm sure it had a lot to do with how good that shit felt. How submissive she was to my control. How wet she'd get for me. But more than that it had to do with the fact that when I was inside of her I felt whole. The act of filling her made *me* feel whole. Nothing or no one had ever made me feel like that before.

Nothing or no one had ever made me feel like I belonged. Charlie made me feel like I belonged inside of her. Like I belonged to her.

I used her hips to help her get used to riding me. Helped her find the rhythm that gave her the most pleasure. I watched her. Watched her enjoy having me inside of her. Watched her head fling back. Her lips tremble as she went up and moan as she went down.

I watched her look down at the connection of us in disbelief. Watched her watch her cream come out of her and saturate me. Watched her circle her hips and find her spot. Her eyes found mine in surprise at how good it felt to her. I couldn't help but smile and lay back. Give myself to her for her use totally and completely.

She went in. Up and down. Side to side. Circling her hips. Slow and long. Fast and hard. Deep. Until her orgasm caught her by surprise. With her being on top it was far more powerful than any she'd had before. I had to sit back up and keep her from falling.

Charlie giggled as her orgasm subsided.

"I love the way you feel inside of me, Knight. You feel so fucking good."

I pulled her down to me for a kiss as I began to thrust up and into her. The added friction had her grabbing my arms and squeezing as she moaned into my mouth.

"This is *my* pussy now," I informed her as I switched positions and placed her on her back. Lifting her ass off the edge of the bed, I continued the friction of our bodies colliding from different directions. Bringing her back and forth onto my dick as I circled my hips. Her legs began to close as she switched between moaning, whimpering, and not being able to make a sound at all.

"This is my good pussy. You're my good thing. You belong to me, Charlie. Do you hear me?"

"Yes!" she screamed as she came and convulsed against me. "Yes, yes, yes, yes, yes," she muttered as I placed her shaking body completely on the bed.

Still going in and out of her until my own release hit me. I stopped moving immediately as I came, but that didn't stop her from squeezing her walls and moving her hips against me. Making me grunt and crash down onto her as my toes curled.

Her arms and legs wrapped around me, as they did every time we finished, and she kissed my neck and face repeatedly as I struggled to catch my breath.

Charlie

The gala was tonight and I had so much to do to get ready. I had to meet with a new client this morning before delivering a post pregnancy package to Evelyn. When I delivered it I ended up being over there for an additional hour because she wanted to talk about Adam and his infidelity. After I left her I had to go to Bundled to take pictures of practically everything in the store for one of my high risk clients. She was only five months and had been placed on bed rest already.

Once I had all of that done I planned on heading home to meet Deja so she could start on my hair and makeup, but Knight wanted me back home… no. What am I saying? That's not my home. That's his home. Knight wanted me to come back to his place, so I told my bestie to meet me over there.

After the day I told him that I'd had I was ready to just take a nap and get ready, but he called and told me that he had an appointment made for me at the spa. Who does that? Who makes you an appointment at the spa and pays for it just because you mentioned to him that you were having a crazy day? Knight Carver.

I came home… I came to *his* home and received the same greeting from him that I'd gotten the day before – him meeting me for a hug and a kiss. Swear I could get used to this. We chilled for a bit before Deja came to work her magic on me.

Now I was sitting in a chair in his living room as she rolled my hair, thinking of something special that I could do for Knight. I crossed my left leg over the right and twisted my mouth in thought. What did he like? Basketball. Going to the gym. From the bookshelf in his closet I gathered that he likes to read. Mostly historical and educational stuff that I'd never think about reading. Maybe I could get him a new book to add to his collection.

"Beauty!" he yelled from his room.

Deja nudged my shoulder and made this weird noise teasing me.

"Shut up, Day," I turned my head to the left some towards the stairs. "What?" I yelled back.

"Is she done yet?"

"She just started, Knight."

"Can you take a break? I need you to find me something to wear."

"You haven't picked anything to wear?"

He was silent. *Too* silent.

"Deja!" he yelled as he completely ignored my question.

"What?" she asked fighting back her laugh.

"Is she coming?"

Deja and I laughed as I stood and made my way to him. I found him in his closet scratching his head, looking from one piece of clothing to the other. I shook my head as I pushed him back gently and stepped in front of him.

"Knight, half of this stuff is brand new with tags on it. Do you go anywhere?"

"Not while I'm home. I go out when I'm on the road, but I buy stuff in whatever city I'm in."

Not finding what I wanted, I turned and looked on the opposite side of his closet. My eyes were captured immediately by red. The same red as the dress I was going to wear. I took a few steps forward and grabbed the jacket to see it up close.

"This is gorgeous. Elegant. Classy…" it was a Sebastian Cruz Couture slim fitting red paisley jacket. It had the baddest flower designs covering the entire jacket. I ran my hand over the satin shawl collar before doing the same to the black pocket square with white trim. "And it's the same color as my dress."

I handed the jacket to him and went over to his shirts.

"You are going to look so sexy in that," and as soon as that thought hit me I was thinking about picking something else for him to wear. Knight would already get lots of attention because of how handsome he was. The last thing I wanted to do was add to his sexiness and be irritated the entire night from women looking at him or even trying to flirt with him. I reached for it as I said, "Maybe we should pick something else."

He laughed as he lifted the jacket out of my reach.

"No, girl. You want me in this, this is what I'm going to wear. Now find me a shirt and some pants. Put it on the bed when you're done."

Knight smacked my ass and left me alone in the closet. I chose a black shirt that he had with white trim and buttons, black pants, and a pair of black Ferragamo loafers. Pleased with what I had, I went over to his bed. I dropped the shoes at the foot of it, then placed the pants and shirt on the bed next to the jacket. And that's when I noticed two plane tickets on top of the jacket.

I looked towards the opened door of the bathroom as I grabbed the tickets.

"Knight?"

"Yea, babe?"

Reading over the date on the tickets, I sat on the bed and allowed a smile to cover my face.

"Midnight tonight," I whispered to myself. "Knight?"

"Yea?"

"You're going to Vegas?"

He came to the bathroom door and leaned against the doorframe.

"*We're* going to Vegas."

"Tonight?"

"Tonight."

I was happy. I was surprised. I was excited. Then I was worried. What about my clients? What about if this doesn't last forever and I get used to this spontaneous, nice, romantic man and feel lost without him?

"What's the matter?" he asked as he walked over to me.

"I can't just up and fly to Vegas tonight and stay until," I looked at the return date. "Monday morning."

"Why not?"

"Well, what about my clients?"

"Didn't you say you wanted to hire an assistant? This weekend would be the perfect time to see how she would do without you. If your clients needed anything from now until Monday she could handle it for you."

That made sense. Brea and I had been talking about her coming to work for me a lot. She already had experience packaging and making deliveries. The only thing she wouldn't be able to do was pamper sessions and deliveries. I didn't have any pampering sessions scheduled for this weekend, and none of my clients were due to go into labor.

What was the point of having my own business, time, and money, not to mention this gorgeous man, if I didn't take advantage of it? If we left tonight, we'd have all of Saturday and Sunday to ourselves before having to return home Monday morning.

Monday morning.

I had to meet with Doctor Berry.

Monday morning.

I was supposed to be going back home.

Fine.

"OK. I can't believe you did this. This is going to be so much fun, Knight. Thank you!"

I jumped into his arms and gave him the reaction he was probably hoping for. Our lips connected long enough to have my panties growing wet before I pulled away.

"I better finish getting ready," I said as he put me down.

"Yea. I agree. Otherwise your best friend is going to hear the sounds you make when I'm deep in that pussy."

"Wow," I turned at the sound of Knight's voice. Deja was running her fingers through my big, loose curls one final time before she left. "You look..." Knight shook his head as he looked me over from head to toe. "Stunning. You're beautiful, Charlie."

I blushed and lowered my head as Deja excused herself.

"Thanks, Knight. You're very handsome tonight. Not that you aren't handsome every night, but that red against your skin just... takes you to another level."

"As it does you."

I looked at myself in the mirror as he walked over to me. The red, sleeveless gown that I wore was tight fitting at the top and loose and flowy at the bottom.

"I hope you're prepared to be reapplying this red lipstick the entire night," he warned me.

"No need. It's lip stain so it won't be coming off any time soon."

"Good."

His lips seized mine and he pulled me into him – letting me feel every inch of what I'd done to him.

"I'm heading out, Lie! Have fun!" Deja yelled from downstairs.

"Thank you!" I replied as I licked Knight off my lips.

He took a step back and readjusted his jacket.

"We need to go before we end up not going at all," Knight grabbed his phone and keys from the dresser. "Have you heard from Harlem? She wanted to come and take pictures before we…"

The door opened and closed again and we heard Harlem talking on the phone. I followed Knight down the stairs anxiously. I could've skipped the gala entirely at this point, but we'd already missed casino night so I wanted to at least go for an hour or two. Harlem ended her call at the sight of Knight, and when he stepped to the side and she saw me she squealed and grabbed Knight's hand.

"Y'all fucked didn't it?"

"*Harlem!*"

Knight pulled his hand away from her as I hung my head, trying and failing horribly at holding my laugh in.

"Excuse me. Y'all had sex didn't it?"

"That ain't none of your damn business crazy ass lil girl!"

"You don't have to tell me. I see it all over Charlie's face."

That got me to lift my head and look from her to Knight.

"What the hell does that mean, Harlem?" Knight asked getting all up in her personal space.

"She's glowing. She has the *I been getting me some di* – she's glowing."

"What you know about glowing from sex?"

Harlem pointed towards her stomach with a confused look on her face and I laughed even harder. Knight looked like he was about to pop a vessel, so I walked over to him and wrapped my arm around his waist.

"Y'all a couple now? You can at *least* tell me that."

"Harlem, you've got about three seconds to take your pictures and get out before I strangle you."

"You wouldn't dare strike a pregnant lady would you?"

He looked at her for all of about two seconds before she was taking our picture. I tried to hide it, but I kind of wanted to hear the answer to that too. *Were* we in a relationship? I mean… I know he said that I belonged to him and all of that… but was that just manly sex talk? Or did he really mean that? I needed to hear him literally say that we were in a relationship before I believed it was real.

KNIGHT

As soon as we made it to the gala I was ready to go, but we knew that we had to make an appearance. The gala was our idea. We had to be here. Two hours was the allotted time we agreed on. We were ten minutes away from that when I fixed us what would be our last drink of the night. I handed Charlie hers and was about to take a sip from mine when I heard someone call my name.

"Coach Frank?" I mumbled as I turned around.

Coach Frank. My high school basketball coach. He was the reason I was in the position I was in today. When I started my ninth grade year he was the assistant coach. The head coach at the time didn't see the talent and potential I had. Because of that, he never had me in the starting lineup.

Coach Frank went to bat for me and made sure that I was in the starting lineup whenever we had scouts in the building. Eventually it became the norm for every game. By my junior year, he was the head coach and I was the captain of the team.

I sat my drink down and we shook hands and hugged.

"Coach Frank, it's good to see you, man. How are you?"

"I'm good. Good. Not as good as you, though. Who is this beautiful woman you have here with you?"

Charlie put her drink down to shake his hand as I introduced them.

"This is my girlfriend Charlie White."

Her head jerked towards me with her mouth open in shock before she closed it and smiled. Coach laughed as I looked down at her in disbelief. My silly ass woman.

"Why are you looking like that, Charlie? What did you think I meant when I told you that you belonged to me?"

She shrugged and removed her hand from Coach's absently.

"I don't know. I mean... I just tho-"

I kissed any doubts she had away before she could even let them fall out of her mouth. When I released her she took a step back and stared at me like she wanted me to throw her on top of the table and have my way with her.

"I meant that shit, Charlie," was all I said.

Charlie licked her lips and nodded before hugging me in that tight way that somehow made me feel free. Only with her. I smiled and kissed her neck as I hugged her back.

"Can we go now?" her arms went from around my neck to my chest. She looked into my eyes as she unbuttoned my jacket. "Please?"

I grabbed her hand and was about to lead her out of the ballroom, but the sight of Coach Frank reminded me that I'd forgotten all about him.

"Shit. My fault, Coach."

"Oh no need. You two have fun."

He tipped his drink at me and winked at Charlie. That was all it took for her to get embarrassed, but she wasn't about to change her mind on me and try to make us stay. I quickly led her out of the ballroom and to my car.

"I'm so embarrassed. He probably thinks I'm crazy."

"He might think you're a little crazy, but he thinks I'm crazy too so that means you're perfect for me."

She giggled and wrapped her arms around mine as we rushed to the car.

Charlie

Vegas was amazing! It wasn't my first time visiting, but it was my first time visiting and feeling so alive and free. I returned to Memphis filled with love and positivity that I believed no one could pull me out of – until I walked into Doctor Berry's office.

He offered me the seat across from his and released a loud, stressed breath as he sat down. My heart began to beat at a more rapid pace as I watched him tap his pen on his desk while he stared at me. As if he was trying to figure out how he was going to say whatever it is he called me in to say.

During our stay in Vegas, Knight and I showered together. During that shower things got a little heated, which led to me being pushed under the shower head. The semi straight hair that I was enjoying for the past few days was now gone and replaced with my natural curls. I had it all pulled up into the bun I'd put it in after our shower. It's a shame to say, but I can't do much of anything with my hair when it's in its natural state. It's too much of it. Too wild. Too big. Too full. Too long. Too curly. But I love it. And so does Knight.

Anyway, I squeezed at the ball on the top of my head about five times before Doctor Berry placed the pen on his desk and cupped his hands together. He sighed again and shook his head. Would he just spill it already??? What could he possibly have to tell me that he was dreading this much? Couldn't have been anything about my health. My family. What was the freaking problem?

"Charlie, there's something that you should know. Something that you should've known a long time ago. I… we never thought it would matter, so that's why I never said anything. I can't speak for anyone else."

"Just tell me what you have to tell me, Dr. Berry."

He rubbed his hand over his face and sighed again.

"Do you know Knight's family? His mother?"

"I know his youngest sister. Harlem. I know that he has another one, but I've never met her before. Or his father. And I know that his mother died years ago. Why? Is something wrong with Knight?"

He scratched the bridge of his nose and looked towards the door.

"No, Charlie," his eyes returned to me. "Do you know his mother's name? When she died? *How* she died?"

Growing frustrated with this 20 questions game, I sat up in my seat and placed my hand on his desk.

"Just tell me what you have to tell me," I repeated with more sternness in my voice than before.

"His mother died 10 years ago. Same day of your heart surgery," not catching the connection I continued to stare at him in silence. "His mother was Angela. Angela Carver."

What

The

Fuck.

Not *my* Angela.

Not the Angela who chose me.

Who gave me her heart.

No.

That

That couldn't have been his mother.

How could I have not put two and two together with them having the last name?

"Angela? His mother's name is Angela?"

My heartbeats sped up. They grew harder. My heart thumped against my rib cage wildly. And my breathing came out just as fast and hard. Trying not to go into a panic, I pushed my seat back and leaned forward.

"Not my Angela. Not the one who gave me her heart," I looked at him with pleading eyes. "This is another Angela Carver. Right? Not the same one."

His silence was my answer along with his hung head. All of the open space that was in his office before began to close around me. The walls grew tighter and tighter. Pulled themselves around me closer and closer.

"Oh my God."

I stood and paced around the suddenly way too small space.

"How could this be? He's... he's not going to want to have anything to do with me."

My chest started rising and falling harder. Quicker. My heart started beating harder. Quicker. So quick I started feeling like it was going to explode. I felt like I couldn't breathe. Short choppy breaths came out in spurts feeling like they were going to strangle me. My hands began to sweat and shake, and before I could stop them tears were streaming down my face.

Doctor Berry stood and walked over to me. He grabbed my shoulder and led me back to my seat.

"Relax, Charlie. Calm down before you have a panic attack."

"But. He. He. I didn't. Dr. Berry. I."

My words just like my lungs were failing me. I couldn't breathe. I couldn't breathe. I grabbed my neck and tried not to let my emotions overpower me.

Doctor Berry's hand went to the middle of my back and he pushed, causing me to lower my head between my legs.

"Close your eyes and take long, slow breaths for me, Charlie. Breathe. Breathe. Nice and slow. Inhale two lungs full of air for me. Long and slow, Charlie."

Forcing my lungs to open again, I did as Doctor Berry asked, and after about five deep breaths my breathing had returned to normal.

"That's it. Just relax."

I palmed my face and continued to breathe as my legs shook. When my heartbeats returned to normal I sat back in my seat and inhaled deeply one last time.

"I see your breathing is back to normal. Let me check your heart."

Doctor Berry pulled his stethoscope from around his neck as I shook my head.

"That's not necessary, Dr. Berry, I'm..."

Before I could finish he was listening to my heart.

"Give me a deep breath in, Charlie," I did. "And exhale," I did. "Inhale," I did. "Exhale."

I did. Pleased with what he heard, he stood and returned to his seat. He didn't speak right away, and I didn't mind now. I didn't mind the silence. I didn't mind it one bit.

"Are you going to tell him, Charlie? He doesn't know just like you didn't."

Should I? Maybe things would be best if I didn't tell him. What if he breaks up with me? Am I willing to risk not having him anymore just to tell the truth? A truth he isn't asking for? But should I risk losing him by keeping it from him?

"Why'd you have to tell me?" I grabbed my purse off the floor and stood. "Why couldn't you just let me stay in my perfect little happy loving bubble?"

Doctor Berry smiled as he stood.

"Because I care about you and I didn't want you to find out in any other way. Knight took losing his mother very hard. He was angry. Very angry. With God. With her. His father. Her doctor. I'm just... not sure how he's going to react to you having his mother's heart. I wanted you to be prepared."

"Well... thank you."

"Are you going to tell him?"

My middle and ring fingers ran down my scar as I walked towards his door.

"I guess so. Eventually. I should. I am."

Doctor Berry nodded and placed his stethoscope back around his neck. He walked to his door and opened it for me. We walked out and started down the hall when Knight called me.

"This is him. I'll see you later, Dr. Berry."

"Be careful, Charlie. And please... know that I didn't mean any harm."

"Oh no. That's... I know you told me because you care about me and I appreciate it honestly. It's just... a hard pill that I'm struggling to swallow right now, but I will."

"OK. I'll let you get to your call."

I nodded and waited until he was a few steps away before I answered.

"Hi."

"What's up?"

"About to head to my first client of the day. What you doing?"

"Just got off the phone with Ozart Raid."

His name sounded familiar, but I couldn't place where I knew it from. I started walking down the hall as I repeated the name over and over in my head.

"Ozart Raid. Why does that sound familiar?"

"He's a retired coach. Used to be the Grizzlies coach before he retired."

"Right. Right. What did he want?"

"He wants me to announce a charity basketball game he's having in New York."

"That's great, babe! When is it?"

"Two weekends away."

The pout that was about to cover my face faded away when I stepped outside and felt the sun's rays shining down on me. I smiled and looked around the parking lot for my car.

"Oh. How long will you be gone?"

"Just the weekend. I'll leave Friday and be back late Sunday night."

"That's not too bad. I guess I can be without you."

He chuckled deep in his throat and I bit down on my lip.

"Listen... I was thinking."

"About?"

After unlocking my car, I tossed my purse in the backseat and got in – making no effort to start the car until our conversation was over.

"I should meet your family before I go," I didn't realize I hadn't answered him until he spoke again. "Charlie?"

"Huh?"

"I said I should meet your family before I go."

"Yea. Yea. Sure. Um... you... you really want to do that? That means things are getting serious doesn't it?"

"They are. For me."

My smile was tortured as I rested my forehead on the steering wheel. I should just tell him now. I should just tell him now and get it out the way. Just tell him now and let him decide what to do with it. What to do with us.

"Me too."

The hell? I lifted my head and smacked my own damn forehead.

"So… you should make that happen, beauty. I don't wanna be just some random that your family has no idea about. I want them to know who I am to you because I'm going to make sure my family knows who you are to me."

That was it. There was no way I could tell him at this point. At least not right now.

"I would like that, Knight. A lot. I really like you. So much."

"I like you. Bring your ass when you're done working."

⟩ KNIGHT ⟨

I did not plan on spending my Friday afternoon going over to Tage's house. He showed up at my doorstep this afternoon with Harlem. Let her tell it she had no idea he was going to be here waiting for her. I'd been letting her drive my spare car, so when she pulled up he was pulling up right behind her.

She hadn't been talking to him at school or when she was at home, so he took the initiative to follow her home and force her to talk to him. I gave him points for that, and when he asked to speak with me he earned even more.

Tage said that he wanted to go ahead and tell his parents about the baby. He was ready to step up. He wanted to be there with Harlem every step of the way. I was all for it and even offered to be there for him.

When we got to his home he was visibly nervous. Like fidgeting nervous. Sensing his nervous energy, I kept Harlem behind me and walked a little in front of Tage as well. For whatever reason he was really afraid of telling his parents, and I wanted him to know that I was going to be there for him no matter how it played out.

Tage's mother, Patricia, led us into the living room before going to get his father, Everett. His mother seemed to have no idea what the hell was going on, but the second his father walked in and saw Harlem and I his head flung back and he shook it adamantly.

Patricia grabbed his arm and led him to the couch that was across from me and Harlem. Tage was sitting next to Harlem, but when his father came in he put some space between them.

"Well, to what do we owe the pleasure of," Patricia gestured between me and Harlem, "This."

I looked around the room at all of the trophies with Tage's name on them. All of the pictures of him in his football uniform. From little league looked like to now. He was deep with his craft. Looked like he was pretty good at it too.

His head lowered as he mumbled, "As you can see..." he looked at Harlem's protruding stomach and she placed her hand over it. "She's pregnant."

"What does that have to do with you?" Everett asked.

I inhaled deeply and sat back in my seat.

Tage grabbed Harlem's hand. She looked at him like she wanted to snatch it away, but she placed her other hand on top of his to show him her support. Even if her petty ass *was* still mad at him.

"It's mine."

"What's yours?" Patricia asked.

"The baby, Ma. She's pregnant with my baby."

"Are you sure?" Patricia asked as Everett said, "Are you stupid? How many times have I told you to keep your fucking dick in your pants, Tage? You have your entire future ahead of you and plenty of time for sex and women later in life. Now was supposed to be about school and football. How are you going to focus on college and get into the NFL with this hanging over you?" he turned towards Harlem and I sat up immediately at the hostile look on his face. "She's probably just trying to trap you because she knows how talented you are."

Harlem chuckled as I interjected.

"See, that's what we're not about to do. You're not about to disrespect her."

"And who are you?"

"That doesn't matter right now. I get that you're upset, but you will not disrespect her."

Harlem grabbed my arm and pulled me back into the couch. Dismissing me, he looked towards Tage.

"Why did you wait so late to say something? We could've paid her off and gotten her to get rid of it. How far along is she?"

"OK, you know what? I'll see you later, Tage," Harlem stood and looked down at me. "Let's go, Knight. I don't have time for this."

I stood and looked at Tage. His head was practically in his lap it was hanging so low. I walked over to him and grabbed his shoulder.

"We'll get through this together," I told him.

He nodded and smiled with half of his mouth as his father started in again.

"He's not getting through anything. His focus is school and football. He doesn't have time to make anything else a priority. Not her and for damn sure not that bastard child she's carrying."

I chuckled and turned towards him as Harlem grabbed my hand and tried to pull me away.

"I'm going to let that slide because I know you're upset," I warned him, pulling away from Harlem's grip. "But if you say anything to disrespect my sister or my nephew from this point forward, I'm going to punch the words back into your mouth."

Everett stood and Patricia stood right along with him. Trying and failing to sit him back down. He stepped in front of me and Tage stood next to me.

"Fuck you, her, and that bas-"

I snapped. Snapped. Can't really remember even hitting him or how many times I hit him, but by the time I was done Tage and Harlem were dragging me out and my knuckles were bleeding.

Patricia was yelling and screaming about calling the police.

He was knocked the hell out.

Tage was looking like I'd done him a favor.

And Harlem... Harlem just kept shaking her head.

I yanked away from the both of them and walked to the car in front of them, only to stop and return to Tage.

"I get why you didn't want to tell him. He's an asshole. But as a man you are *required* to stand up and take care of your responsibilities. Just as I told Harlem, this baby is not going to stop her from becoming the woman she planned on being. The same goes for you. Just because she's pregnant does not mean your life is over. That your dreams have to be altered. As long as you put forth the effort to be there for her and your child I will be there with y'all every step of the way."

He nodded and looked back towards his house. His hand extended for mine and I shook it.

"Thanks, man. You're right. I'll be there no matter what."

I nodded as I wiped the blood off of my knuckles onto my shirt.

"I'll give you two a second."

I went to the car and waited for Harlem. I wanted to give them their space, but I also wanted to make sure Everett didn't try to come out, so I glanced up at them every few seconds. By the end of their conversation Tage was pulling Harlem into him for a hug that she willingly accepted. As she walked to my car he walked to his.

"Where is he going?" I asked after she closed the door.

"To his brother's house. Their father is very controlling... and he drinks. And when he drinks he's even more of an asshole."

Normally I'd check her for cursing, but this time... asshole was the perfect word to describe him.

"Just... be careful," I heard Harlem mutter after letting Charlie in.

I was in my room laying on the bed. Had been in that same position for about three hours. Just staring at the ceiling. No music. No TV. No talking. Just staring. Staring and thinking. Trying to understand what made me snap and come apart as easily as I did.

All of my years in the gym, at the punching bag, in the boxing ring... was meant to help me avoid this. It was no secret to me that I had anger issues. That I was fiercely protective of my family. But today... today showed me that I didn't have it together as well I thought I did.

"Be careful?" I heard the smile in Charlie's voice, and it made me smile for the first time since I'd gotten back home. "Why?"

"That's not the first time I've seen Knight fight. Hell, he used to beat people up for me and Carmen all the time, but today was different. That wasn't just him being mad at Everett talking about me and the baby. That was... some pent up shit that he let loose."

"Thanks for the warning. How's my baby?"

"He's good. Kicking the shit out of me."

"Can I?"

"Sure."

Not being able to see them had me imagining what was happening. I figured Charlie had her hand on Harlem's stomach to see if Hayden would move. The house felt like it grew completely still as we waited. Waited to see if Hayden would act right or be stubborn like the family he'd been born into.

"Ah! He kicked, Harlem!"

Harlem laughed and so did I.

"I know. I felt it too."

"Oh yea. Duh," Charlie chuckled as she finally made her way to me. "I'll see you a little later. Have you been drinking your water?"

"*Yes*, Charlie."

Charlie's head peeked into my room as she smiled. I was waiting for her, but apparently she was waiting for me. She stood there looking around my room until I said...

"Come here, silly."

She scurried over to my bed, kicked her shoes off, and took her jeans and button down off before climbing into bed with me. Her body snuggled up on the side of me, and I swear, wrapping my arm around her and kissing her felt like the most natural thing to me.

"You wanna talk about it," Charlie's hand lifted mine. Her lips kissed my bruised knuckles softly. One by one. "But we don't have to if you don't want to."

"There's nothing to talk about really. I just snapped."

"But why? I mean... from what Harlem told me earlier today and just a few seconds ago... all it would've taken was one punch to prove your point. To teach him a lesson for disrespecting her and the baby, but you didn't stop. Why didn't you stop?"

She sat up on her elbow while running her hand up and down my chest. The feel of her hand against my skin was helping me stay calm, but I was still growing irritated just at the thought of it. Not so much over Everett, but irritated at myself for giving him the power to make me step out of my character like that.

"What do you want me to say, Charlie? You want me to say I lost control? I did."

"But why?"

With a loud exhale, I pushed her hand off of my body and sat on the edge of the bed.

"I don't know, Charlie. He just pissed me off. If you think I was wrong for standing up for my family..."

"No," her hand wrapped around my arm as best as it could and she pulled me back down to the bed. "That's not what I'm saying at all, Knight. I think that was very noble of you. Not only were you standing up for their honor, but you stood up for Tage too. I'll never go against you for doing that. I just," her eyes darted over to the other side of the room as she chewed on her cheek. "Want to know what triggered you not being able to keep control of yourself. Maybe I can help you with that. When she called me and told me what happened the first thing I thought was what if they couldn't have stopped you? What if you would've done some serious damage or killed him? What if they would've called the police and…"

"You were scared of losing me?"

Her watery eyes were my answer. She smiled softly and shook her head.

"Is that selfish of me?"

Now I was the one shaking my head as I pulled her down to my lips. This is what I've needed *all* fucking day. *Her*.

"That's not selfish. Honestly, it makes me feel good as hell, Charlie."

And it also made me want to try and figure this out with her. I didn't want her to ever have to worry about losing me; especially because I lost my temper and snapped on someone. She placed her head in the middle of my chest. On my heart. I knew then and there that it would always be hers.

"I guess maybe that was me unleashing a lot of anger that has been stored up."

"From what? Losing your mom?"

"Everything, beauty. I was so angry. I know I might sound like a broken record. I know you probably think I should just get over it…"

"No, Knight. I... I can't say that I understand how you feel, but I understand grief. I had to watch my family grieve over me and I wasn't even gone yet. I had to watch them plan my funeral. My mother fought them every step of the way, but they had the entire ceremony planned. We all handle loss differently and I honestly think you haven't handled losing your mother at all.

I think you've stuffed it down in the deepest, darkest place you could find in your heart. And it's just... festering. It's been festering all of these years because you haven't dealt with it. You haven't wanted to feel that pain. So you've been feeling anger instead."

Now that was true. Anger I definitely allowed myself to feel. I was mad at God for taking her. Mad at her for leaving. Mad at my pops for not trying to make her stay. Mad at Carmen for moving. Mad at Harlem for being so damn young. But above all I was mad at myself for not doing what she asked of me. For not being around when her health deteriorated.

Anger I definitely allowed myself to feel.

"You need to get it out, Knight. I'm more than willing to listen while you do."

We turned on our sides to face each other, but I couldn't speak right away. She was asking me to dig up 10 years of anger. 10 years of hurt. 10 years of guilt. Where would I even start? Where would she put it? My feelings. What would she do with them? Carry them around with her?

"I don't want to put all of this on you, Charlie. I wouldn't even know where to start. Where to end. This would take all night probably longer."

She smiled as she ran her hand down the back of my head.

"For you... I have all the time in the world."

Charlie

Tonight was nerve racking for two reasons. One – I'd never brought a man home to meet my family. More than anything, I've had men brought home for me. Men that I've never been interested in. But I've never in my life brought a man home to meet my family.

Two – this made things between us real. I mean, I knew that things between us were real, but this makes them *really* real. It lets me know that Knight is committed to us. That he sees a future with me.

And knowing that I know something that he doesn't makes me feel like shit.

I've longed to tell him that I have his mother's heart ever since I found out, but I'm so freaking scared. It's no secret that he's felt all types of feelings over losing his mother. Guilt. Anger. Hurt. I'm just scared that he'll look at me differently.

Pushing that disturbing thought from my head, I left my hiding place, the bathroom, and went back into the kitchen with my mom and sister. It wasn't that I didn't want to be around them because I loved them dearly. It's just... they were acting so weird about Knight coming over.

They were all googly eyed and smiley faced the entire time we cooked. Asking me the most random, unnecessary things about him. Constantly asking me what time he was going to be here like I hadn't already told them a million times. Six o'clock. Six o'clock. Six o'clock.

"Charlie..."

"Six o'clock," I said quickly cutting my mom off.

"Not that, Lie. I... can I see you in my room for a second?"

I followed my mom into her room and became a little alarmed when she stepped behind me and closed the door.

"Is something wrong, Ma?"

Her smile was sweet as she hugged me from the side and took me over to her vanity. That vanity had gotten me into lots of trouble as a young girl. All of her makeup and perfumes were on and in that vanity, and I had been fascinated with it since the age of four. I broke bad at six and made my face up just like I'd watched her do many times. Of course mine didn't come out anything like hers.

She thought it was so cute and funny until she saw the mess I'd made.

And not to mention the fact that I'd drenched myself in almost her whole bottle of White Diamonds.

I would get into her vanity every chance I could. So much so that she had a new handle put on her door that locked from the outside and inside to keep me from getting in alone.

My mom positioned me in front of the vanity and pulled on my arms, signaling she wanted me to sit. Just as soon as I was close enough my fingers started running across the white antique vanity. Out of reflex I picked up her bottle of White Diamonds and was about to spray it on myself, but I thought about Knight and kept my scent the way he liked it.

She smiled and kissed my temple. Her hands went to my shoulders as I looked at her through the mirror.

"This was your great-grandmother's vanity. She passed it along to your grandmother. Who passed it down to me. I was supposed to give it to Veronica on her 18th birthday, but she knew how much you love this thing, so she told me that day that she wanted you to have it on yours. You remember what we were doing on your 18th birthday, Charlie?"

How could I forget? I'd spent the entire week in the hospital. I nodded and lowered my head naturally at the thought, but she lifted it and continued to look at me through the mirror.

"I guess I've kept it since then because… every time I look at it, it reminds me of my little beautiful baby girl. Coming into this room and finding your little seven-year-old feet in my size seven shoes," we both shared a chuckle at the visual. "Bold red lipstick all over your lips and chin. And you would always put the lightest eyeshadow on that you could find. But you were still the most beautiful girl in the world to me."

I turned in the seat to face her.

"I kept it, Charlie, because… if anything were to ever happen to you… I'd have this to remember you by. The healthy, innocent you."

"Ma, nothing's going to happen to me."

She nodded and grabbed my hand. I stood as she struggled to find the right words to say.

"I know that now, baby. I really do. It's just that this is… 10 years, Charlie. I… I said I'd wait until we reached this point to give it to you. So, whenever you want, your father or brother can bring it to your place for you."

"Really? I can have it?"

"Really. It's yours."

I looked back at the vanity before grabbing her and pulling her into me for a hug.

"Thanks, Ma. This is just… great. You don't know how much this means to me."

"You don't know how much *you* mean to me. I love you *so much*, Charlie."

"I love you too, Ma."

We released each other and she wiped her eyes. The ringing of the doorbell signaled my man's arrival. I smiled against my will. He always had that effect on me. Smiling… I've always done that… but with Knight… they felt different. They came from a different place. A different emotion. I've been joyful all of my life.

If sickness teaches you anything it teaches you to not let anything or anyone steal your joy. That God is in control and He has the final say. It teaches you that in your weakness He is your strength. That what you can do on your own in no way compares to what He can do through you.

But with Knight... I was just straight up happy. Just... giddy. And in love. Wait... what?

"Well, let's go meet this young man," she said as she walked out of the room.

I stood there for a second. Trying to come to grips with my thoughts. My feelings. Was I in love with Knight? Like really in love with Knight? Smoothing my shirt with my hands, I pulled the hem of it gently before heading out of the room.

I made it into the living room... and the sight of him standing in the middle of the father and brother... smiling and nodding as he listened to what my father was saying closely. His hand was on top of Knight's shoulder... like he'd been knowing him for years.

Knight looked up at me. His smile widened. Mine did too.

"Hi," I spoke as he took a step away from them and focused completely on me.

"What's up?"

⟩ KNIGHT ⟨

She didn't think I'd picked up on it, but Charlie was slowly crawling back into the guarded hole she was in before the auction. Before I claimed her. It was subtle. So subtle a man who hadn't taken the time to study his woman and truly get to know her wouldn't have been able to pick up on it. But I knew her. And I knew that she was shutting down on me.

It started with her being too busy to come over during the day. She'd come over late and all we'd do is eat, maybe have sex, and go to sleep. She didn't want to talk. When the sun was up so was she. Forgetting to pack a bag so she'd have to rush home to get ready for her day.

Instead of doing things with Harlem in the house to get ready for the baby, she'd pick her up, take her wherever they needed to go, drop her off, and leave. Her excuse was that she had other clients, but before I met her family she'd always take care of Harlem last to spend the rest of her day and night with us.

Our phone calls were few and far in between, and her text messages were growing shorter and shorter.

To be honest, I was surprised she even agreed to go out tonight. I wasn't sure if things were moving too fast for her or if this was something she no longer wanted or what. Without talking to her I could only assume, and at this point I was assuming the worst.

We pulled up to the bowling alley and I let out a frustrated sigh as I cut the car off. She was sitting over there twiddling with her thumbs like she was nervous or some shit. Like we hadn't spent practically every day together since we'd met for the past two months. Except for when she called herself putting space between us. I wasn't planning on seeing her at Sticks that night, but we immediately cut that bullshit out.

"What's the problem, Charlie?"

Her eyes met mine briefly before she looked out of the window.

"What do you mean?"

"I'm not... Charlie, I'm not going to play with your ass. If you don't want to be with me... here or otherwise say that shit. But don't shut down on me and act like nothing is going on between us. I'm not stupid."

"I don't know what you're talking about."

"Fine."

I put my hand back on the key in the ignition and was about to turn it to start my car again, but she stopped me.

"I don't want to go."

"But you don't seem like you want to be here. Be with me."

"I do. I want nothing more than to be here with you."

"Then what's the fucking problem?"

She pulled her hand from mine and massaged her forehead.

"It's nothing, Knight. Really. I'm sorry if I've made you feel like I don't want to be with you I really do. I promise I do. I just... have a lot on my mind these days. My business is taking off and I have a lot on my shoulders. It's just a lot right now. And I'm looking for wholesalers and a storefront and I've just been very distracted. I'm sorry."

I didn't believe her, but if she didn't want to tell me the truth I couldn't force her to. Dropping it for now, we went into the bowling alley and immediately grabbed food and drinks. More drinks than food. Her eyes started to lower and she had that sleepy wasted look that was sexy as hell to me. She could hardly ever hold her liquor. Two drinks would have her like this. Three would have her completely gone. It was cute as hell.

Charlie jumped out of her chair and walked over to me. No matter how irritated I got I couldn't ignore the fact that I was irritated because I was crazy about this girl, and I wanted her to be just as crazy about me. I wanted her to want me as much as I wanted her. And the thought of that not being the case was messing with my mental.

None of that mattered when she was this close, though. She grabbed two handfuls of my shirt as I pushed her hair away from her face and grabbed her cheeks.

"I wanna kiss you," she whispered into my lips, "But you're mad at me."

"I'm not mad at you, Charlie. I could never stay mad at you."

She brushed her lips against mine twice before pulling away and looking into my eyes. Like she was trying to see how I'd react to her. My way of showing her – pulling her in for another kiss. A deeper kiss. A longer kiss. She pulled away again and hugged me.

"I promise I want to be with you, Knight. Please, don't doubt that."

I kissed her cheek and removed her arms from around me. Saying OK or that I believed her at this point would be a lie. It wasn't OK and I didn't believe her, so I said nothing at all. We went over to our lane, and the way she was wobbling told me that bowling might not be the move while she had her drinks in her.

"Charlie... you uh... you sure you wanna do this, babe?"

Her head flung back and she exhaled a hard breath with a roll of her eyes like I was annoying her. I laughed as I sat down and watched her struggle to pick up her ball.

"Yes, Knight. I can do this. I can do all things through Christ who is my strength."

"So... you're just going to quote bible scriptures while you're drunk? That's what we're doing now?"

"I am not drunk. I'm a little tipsy, but I'm not drunk."

"Right. Have at it then."

Charlie stood there for a few seconds more, looking from one ball to the other, before picking hers up, dropping it, and giggling as she chased after it sideways. I laughed as I picked her up with one arm and grabbed the ball with my other hand.

"Ima put you at the lane and you just roll the ball, Charlie."

"You are so strong, Knight," she bit down on her lip as she stared at the side of my face. "You're so freaking sexy too. And you're *my* man?"

"Shut up, Charlie."

"Are you blushing?" she grabbed my face but I fought against her because I was blushing and looking at her would only make it worse. "You *are* blushing. Awww, Knight!"

Her lips on my neck had me rethinking this bowling thing again. I was tempted to take her to the car and take her, but I was enjoying the sight of tipsy Charlie way too much to end it just yet. At the lane, I placed her on her feet. She wobbled slightly and smiled as she tried to gain her balance.

"Your tolerance is weak as hell, Charlie. I'm just trying to figure out how you're drunk off two drinks."

"I'm not drunk! I'm…"

"Tipsy. Right."

I handed her the ball and walked backwards to my seat. She took a few steps back, did this cute little Flintstone shimmy, ran down the lane, and busted her ass. I'm talking about she straight up ran past the line, went over onto the lane, and slipped and fell! Her uncoordinated ass dropped the ball on the opposite lane, sending it down the gutter while she laughed hysterically at her own self.

I ran over to help her and ended up falling myself, but I didn't care. I just wanted to make sure her crazy ass was good. We sat there, in the middle of this crowded bowling alley, laughing as if we had not one care in the world.

"Why did you pass the line and do down the lane, Charlie? You know it's slippery," I asked when I was finally able to stop laughing.

It took her a few seconds more to stop laughing. Tears were streaming down her face as she grabbed my shirt. I wiped them as she smiled and stared into my eyes.

"You fell for me," she whispered.

In more ways than one. My smile softened as I caressed her cheek.

"Wouldn't be the first time."

She kissed me and sighed as her head shook.

"Knight…"

"No, it's… we don't have to go there, Charlie. It's fine."

With a nod she pulled away from me and looked around at all of the people that were staring at us.

"You make it so easy to fall for you, Knight. So easy."

Charlie got on her knees, then put her hands on the floor. She steadied herself and stood. Looking down at me, she extended her hand to help me get up. But there was something about it that seemed… cryptic. Like she would be helping me get up from a different fall. Falling for her. And that fall was one I didn't want to get up from.

Charlie

I lied. Well, I didn't really lie. I just didn't tell Knight the whole truth. Last night at the bowling alley when he asked what the problem was I wasn't completely honest. My workload had picked up quite a bit since I quit at Bundled, but I was kind of avoiding him. It wasn't because I didn't want to be around him.

It was the guilt. The gnawing guilt of wanting to tell him about me having his mother's heart. It was the fear. The nagging fear of losing him when he found out. It was me trying to keep the words from slipping out of my mouth. Me trying not to have to ever experience his anger directed towards me.

Knight was leaving today for the charity basketball game, and I was going to take full advantage of this space we were going to have. There was no way I'd be able to continue to be like this and he let me get away with it. He'd already called me out on it once and I was sure he'd have no problem calling me out on it again. While he was gone, I planned on getting myself together. When he came back I was going to tell him or get back to the way things were.

But there would be no more of this pulling away from him.

Period.

I walked him out to his rental car and was surprised when he handed me the keys to his Lincoln. My forehead went into the center of his chest as I hugged him.

"You're really letting me drive your car?" I asked in disbelief.

"Yes. I must really like you. Ion let nobody drive my cars."

"You let Harlem drive the Charger."

"That's because I don't drive it anymore. Her ass won't be driving the Lincoln."

Looking into his eyes was pure ecstasy. I wanted to know the man behind those eyes the moment they looked into mine. The moment he pierced me with them. And the man that he showed me was nothing like what I was expecting. He was so much better.

"Will you call one of us and let us know you've made it?"

Knight nodded then kissed my forehead. He leaned against his rental, pulling me into his body and wrapping those strong chestnut brown arms around me along the way.

"Are you gonna stay here with her while I'm gone?"

"Do you want me to?"

"Yea. I don't know if it's the hormones or what but she's been a little emotional lately. I think it'll do her some good to have you around. She talks to you more than she talks to me."

"I'll stay then."

"So that means you'll be here when I get back?" those hands… he ran those hands down my back and squeezed my ass. "You don't know what having you here does to my soul. Every time I come home to the both of you…"

His hands went from my bottom set of cheeks to the ones on my face. I watched in heavy anticipation as his head lowered to mine. His tongue was in my mouth quicker than it ever had been and I savored the feel of it until he pulled away.

"You spoil us," he mumbled as he pushed me away.

"I love being here with the two of you."

That was true. It was like we had our own little family thing going on. On my light days I'd cook and we'd play games or watch movies. On my heavy days they would have food ready when I came home. No. I have got to stop saying that. When I came over. Harlem and I shopped and talked and just… vibed. She was like the little sister I always wanted.

"And I don't spoil y'all. I have nothing to spoil you with," I continued.

"You spoil us with you. With your love. Your energy. Your attention. Your affection. You're like... the sunshine we've lacked after years of cloudy days."

"Knight..." the steps I took away from him were stopped by his hand grabbing my shirt and pulling me back into him. "That's really sweet. You're about to make me cry."

"It's the truth, but I don't want you to cry so I'll head out."

"But now I really don't want you to go."

I wanted to jump on him, but I would've hit my knees on the car since his back was against it. As if he was reading my mind, Knight pushed himself off the car and wrapped my legs around his waist.

"I can see now you walking me to the car was not a good idea. Ima have to take you back in the house if I plan on leaving any time soon."

I chuckled and caressed the back of his head and neck as he carried me. His groans as I kissed all over his face and neck had my pussy soaking wet but it didn't matter. There was nothing he could do about it now.

Knight let me kiss him a few times more before putting me on my feet and prying my arms from around his neck. He kissed me quickly then pushed me into the house softly.

"Go," he ordered, shoving his hands into his pockets.

"But..."

"Go, Charlie. Before I change my mind and not take this flight."

"Fine."

I slammed the door in his face and leaned against it, smiling at the sound of him laughing as he walked away. My phone chimed in my pocket, so I pulled it out to read the text as I went back into Harlem's room

My Knight: You gon pay for slamming the door in my face when I get back.

Looking forward to it ;)

Today was the day for Harlem's first pampering session. I was sure she'd be just like my other clients – wanting one every two weeks by the end of this one.

"You ready?" I asked as I entered her room.

"Yep!"

Harlem hopped out of her bed and sat in the chair I had for her. I went to the bathroom to fill my foot massager and a bowl for her hands. When I returned she looked at me like she wanted to say something but was holding it in.

If she wasn't ready to ask or tell I wouldn't force her to. I put her feet in the water and stood to get my brushes, scrubs, and butters out of my bag. She chose my chocolate mint scrub and body butter, so I put the rest in my bag and started her pedicure. I was at the point of scrubbing her left foot with the brush when she called my name.

"Charlie?"

"Yea?"

"Do you love my brother?"

The brush stopped in my hand as I looked up at her with a smirk.

"Is that a trick question?"

She shrugged.

I returned my attention to her foot. Was I ready to have this conversation yet? Was I ready to acknowledge how I felt?

"I was just wondering. Like... I don't know like..." I looked at her again as she drummed her fingers on her thighs. "I don't know what love is or what it looks like. So I was just wondering if you and Knight loved each other. If you all were my example of what love should be like. I'm trying to figure out how I feel about Tage but I don't know what love is. Not this kind of love anyway."

Her confession tugged at the strings of my heart so hard I literally felt myself being pulled towards her with each word she spoke. I put the brush in the water and grabbed the towel to dry my hands and her feet.

"Come... sit with me, Harlem."

We went into the den and sat next to each other. I wanted to see her face, so I turned slightly and pulled my left leg onto the couch.

"OK, so... there are eight different types of love," I started. "Let's see if I can remember all eight. I did a paper on it for my psychology class in college and that feels like forever ago," my eyes closed as I tried to remember all that I'd learned during my studying. "There's eros which is Greek for erotic. It's... it's passion and sexual desire. Impulsive. Intense. Dangerous. It involves a lack of self-control. It's powerful... but it's so superficial that it can burn out quickly. It's extremely selfish as it focuses on physical pleasure, lust, and infatuation. Its focus is on the body.

The second is philia. Affectionate, brotherly love. It's the love we have for friends and neighbors. It isn't a romantic love nor does there have to be physical attraction. It's loyalty and connection without romantic intimacy. Its focus is on the mind.

There's storge or familiar love. It's a natural affection and bond shared between family. Mother and child. Siblings. Childhood friends. It's powerful just as eros love is, but because it's not focused on self-gratification it's a healthier form of love. It can be toxic, though. If your love for your family causes you to do things you shouldn't be, or if you are so worried about them that you don't live for yourself... it can do more harm than good.

Ludus is playful, puppy love. It can have the same intensity and infatuation of eros but it's less about sex and passion and more about feelings and teasing. It's that love you feel when you get butterflies. Or your heart flutters and you get all nervous when he's around. It's innocent, playful, and childlike. Its focus is on emotion.

The fifth kind of love is mania. Obsessive love. It's the kind of love people have when you see them on Snapped. It's extremely dangerous because people who experience this kind of love want to love and be loved so bad that they seek to find their worth and value and esteem in other people. Because of this, they are either possessive, jealous, and hostile... or they feel rejected when the love isn't returned or their worth isn't validated. It makes people dependent. Dependent. Angry. Impulsive. Dangerous.

Pragma, or enduring love, is..."

I smiled as the desire to experience this kind of love with Knight filled me.

"It's love that's lasted and deepened with time. Love that has matured and been through some things and grew stronger because of it. It's love that has been maintained. Fought for. Preserved. Guarded like the treasure that it is.

The last two are two of my favorites.

There's philautia. Self-love. It brings to mind my most necessary scripture to remember. The twenty second chapter of Matthew. Verses thirty-seven through thirty-nine. When Jesus was asked what was the greatest commandment He said to love God with all of your heart, soul, mind, and strength. And He said that the second was like it – to love your neighbor as yourself.

I didn't realize until I was an adult that in order for me to love my neighbor as myself I had to love myself *first*. The order isn't God, others, and then self. The order is God, self, then others.

How can you love your neighbor as yourself if you don't love yourself? Right? So, self-love isn't about being vain or narcissistic. It's not about being selfish and not caring about others. Self-love isn't selfish.

It's the act of knowing yourself. Understanding yourself. Knowing your worth. Seeking your value from God, your Creator, instead of men. It's... accepting yourself and being comfortable in your skin.

Just the way you are.

Embracing those things about you that you cannot change, improving the things you can, and not giving a damn what anyone has to say otherwise.

Self-love is the best way to show your love for others because how can you give what you don't have? You can't love others if you don't love yourself. You'll have nothing to give. Your cup will be empty. Love fills you. You must love God first and let Him fill you with His love, then you pour that love into the hearts and lives us others. Which leads to the last kind of love there is; agape love.

Selfless love. Unconditional love. It's the highest and most sought after yet most misunderstood love of all. It's not conditional. It's not based on what someone can give you or how they make you feel. It's not self-centered. It's focused on action. What you can give to and do for others. It's focused on the person you're loving not yourself. It's not a love that can be earned or one that expects anything in return, but one that must be freely given and received.

Agape love is Godly love. It is the love of God. It's pure. It's gracious and merciful. It doesn't judge. It doesn't expect. It doesn't conform. It's unconditional – flesh, flaws, and all. It accepts. It's a choice. What a person does is irrelevant with agape. When you make that choice to love unconditionally... it's set in stone. It's forgiveness. It's humility. It's our spirit. It's how we connect with God and receive His love and pour it into others.

Do any of those types of love describe how you feel about Tage?"

"No. I guess it started as... what was the playful one? Lupus?"

"Ludus, Harlem."

"Yea that. Now I just can't stand him. I know that he's acting the way he is because of his parents. They had big dreams of him playing in the NFL and setting them up for life. Now they think Hayden is going to ruin that. I guess I'm just mad at myself for wanting him to be around. But I know what it feels like to have both parents and what it doesn't, and if I could do anything to make sure Hayden had both parents in the home I would. I never wanted it to be like this. I wanted to wait until I was married. I just... fucked up."

"Well you definitely don't want to force a relationship with him if you don't really want to be with him. And you can't force him to be there for Hayden if he doesn't want to be. You can put him on child support to make sure he's there financially, but what you don't want to do is cause him to resent Hayden. That baby inside of you deserves to be loved unconditionally. He deserves to be surrounded by genuine love and genuine people. If Tage doesn't want to be around that's his loss; not yours on Hayden's, but I'm going to be completely honest with you, Harlem, I think he's going to come around."

"You do?"

I nodded and grabbed her hand.

"I do. I think he's scared now. I think he just needs time to process everything and come from under his father's thumb. But I definitely think he's going to come around. Don't give up, but don't hold on so hard that you miss out on meeting a good guy. Hayden will have Knight and he's more than enough. Even after Tage comes to his senses."

Harlem hugged my neck and I smiled as I hugged her back.

"Thanks, Charlie. I love you."

"Aww, baby. I love you too."

⋟ KNIGHT ⋞

When I walked into my home it was too quiet. I'd gotten used to random giggling and loud cartoons. Surprisingly, the cartoons were being watched by Charlie most of the time. I wasn't expecting any noise from Harlem because she was spending the night with Princess, but I at least thought Charlie would have on the TV or some music.

Figuring she was sleep, I made my way up the stairs, down the hall, and into my room as quietly as I could. Charlie was so engrossed in whatever the hell she was looking at on her laptop that she didn't even feel my presence until I was in the room and walking towards her.

She immediately slammed her laptop shut and yanked her earbuds out of her ear. Her weirdness... I'd gotten used to... but even this was a little *too* weird for her. I stopped abruptly and looked at her skeptically. Her mouth was partially open until she closed it and swallowed hard.

"Charlie... what are you doing?"

"Nothing," she almost whispered hesitantly.

"Then why..."

"Nothing."

"But I didn't ev–"

"Nothing."

"What's on the computer, Charlie?"

"Nothing."

She put it behind her back and looked everywhere but at me. There was only one thing that made people react this way – porn. But I just... I just refused to believe my girl... my sweet, silly woman was watching porn. There had to be another reason.

"Why are you acting so weird?"

"I'm always weird."

That was true, but this was even more weird than usual.

"I know you're up to something, Charlie."

"Nothing."

I nodded and walked over to my closet to put my bag away for the time being, and when I did I saw a pile of food on the bed. Not just normal food. Strange random food to be eating together. Like cucumbers, bananas, and pickles. The hell kind of freaky shit had she gotten into while I was gone?

"Charlie... what the hell do you have this shit in the bed for? Were you... you were watching porn... weren't you?"

"I was not!" she yelled defensively as she stood and tried to run out of the room but I grabbed her.

"Yes you were! You were watching porn!" I was trying so hard not to laugh because she was visibly embarrassed, but this shit was funny! "Babe, why didn't you tell me you were into that? We could've been watching it together."

"I'm not," she whined, trying to pull away from me. "I just... I'm not going to tell you if you keep laughing at me!"

"All right!"

I turned away from her for a second to try and gather myself. After a few deep breaths I turned to face her and tried my hardest to fight my smile.

"Knight!"

"Dammit, Charlie! You at least gotta let me smile!"

Her eyes closed as she chewed on her cheek.

"Fine. I was watching it... but..." her head shook as she opened her eyes. "But only because I wanted to learn how to... I wanted to learn how to... you know. For you. So I could do it."

"Do what, Charlie?"

"Suck it," she mumbled under her breath.

"Say what?"

"You heard me!"

"No I didn't."

I did. I just wanted her to say it louder.

"Suck. It," she gritted through her teeth.

"Suck what?"

Charlie licked her lips as her eyes lowered. Her embarrassment was quickly being replaced with lust, and I must admit... my dick was growing with each passing second.

"Your dick."

"You actually care that much about pleasing me?"

She nodded and bit down on her lip as she pulled my shirt over my head.

"You wanna see what I learned?"

"*Hell* yea."

I undressed her as she undressed me. The fruit was tossed onto the floor. She stood on the side of the bed and stared at me. Rubbing her chin with her thumb and pointing finger.

"Charlie, you really don't have to do this. I get pleasure from pleasing you. I'm flattered that you even thought enough of it to learn... and practice."

The smile that was spreading on my face had her clamming up again, so I leaned over and pulled her into the bed.

"I wanna do it. I wanna taste you. I've wanted to since our first time."

I couldn't even speak. I wasn't sure if I could speak. I just nodded and leaned back on the headboard. She straddled my legs and looked down at my dick like she'd never seen it before. Her lips started on mine. Kissing them slow but with the right amount of pressure to make me want more. She opened my mouth with her tongue and teased me with it. Pulling it out and licking my lips just when I was about to lose myself in her.

Then she started on my neck. Biting and licking and sucking like this time was her turn to possess me. Like this time was her turn to conquer me. Her hands went down my chest and her lips followed. And when she licked my nipples she introduced me to a pleasure I didn't think I was capable of feeling. Caught me so off guard I damn near pushed her away, but it felt too good so I let her stay.

Her eyes met mine as she kissed her way down my stomach. Pulling me even deeper into her web.

"You'll stop me if I'm doing it wrong, right?"

"Right."

For someone who wanted to feast, Charlie didn't dig in right away. No. She continued the torture of making me wait. Getting close yet so far away. She squeezed my thighs as she stared at my dick. Biting down on her lip. Watching as precum oozed out of me. I was *so* ready for it. Ready for her.

To resist grabbing her hair and putting her where she needed to be, I put my hands behind my head and closed my eyes. The moment I did I felt her tongue on me. I opened my eyes in time enough to watch her run the tip of her tongue across my head – licking my cum up. Then she closed her mouth around it and sucked.

Her eyebrows wrinkled and she paused. Like she was thinking of what to do next.

"Forget what you watched," I coached pulling her eyes up to me. "Do what feels natural. Just no teeth."

With one hand she palmed my balls. The other wrapped around my dick. She took me into her mouth as deep as she could, then ran her tongue over me and sucked her way up with enough pressure to have my thighs clenching.

She did that again. Using her hand to stroke the part of me that she couldn't fit into her mouth. I was out of her mouth and her attention was on my balls, but she continued to stroke me as she licked and sucked them.

"Shit, Charlie."

Her tongue licked every inch of me before she took me back into her mouth. Touching the back of her throat with my head as she looked me dead in my eyes. I don't know if it was what she was doing with her mouth, the fact that she was actually doing it with her mouth, or the combination of both... but I was about to cum quicker than I ever had before.

I grabbed a handful of her hair and tried to control her movements but that didn't help.

"Condom. Now."

Charlie crawled across the bed to the nightstand and grabbed a condom while I got on my knees. She tried to turn around and crawl back to me, but I stopped her and kept her just as she was. Positioning myself behind her, I took the condom from her and got it on as quickly as I could.

I spread her ass cheeks, and the sight of her cream already at her opening made my dick throb. She was ready for me. She was just as turned on by pleasuring me as I get by pleasuring her. I wanted to return the favor, and I definitely would before the night was out, but right now... I just had to feel her.

Charlie looked back at me when I ran my dick against her clit and I smiled.

"Put it in," she ordered softly.

With her back arched perfectly, I slid inside of her, and her moan was the sound I'd been waiting to hear all weekend. But it didn't last long. She grew completely silent. Nothing was heard besides her cream coating me and our bodies connecting.

I felt her walls tightening around me and I pulled out.

"Give it back," she pleaded as her hand came between us.

"If you cum I'll cum and I'm not trying to cum this soon, Charlie."

"I don't care we'll go again. Just give it back."

I slid back inside and looked from me disappearing inside of her and returning to her gripping the sheets and burying her head in the bed. The tightening started again. Her moans started again. Then she was coming. Loud. And long. And hard. And so was I.

Charlie

I don't know what the hell I was thinking when I agreed to meet Knight's family. It was one thing for him to meet mine… but the idea of meeting his father literally turned my stomach. I was so nervous I didn't know what to do with myself! The silver lining was the fact that I wouldn't have to meet his sister Carmen until she returned to Memphis, and I'd been talking to a couple of his closest cousins already, so I kind of felt like I knew them a little.

They were helping me put together a surprise party for his birthday next month, so Harlem linked us up and we've been bouncing ideas off each other for the past few days. With my birthday being this month, I already had my plans for myself made. I felt like Knight had something up his sleeve because he'd been asking a lot of random questions lately, but he hadn't said anything to me about it.

To be honest, the only thing I needed to celebrate another year of life was him. I was just that grateful to have him. Which is the only thing that kept me from getting up and running out of his house before his father arrived. That and the fact that Harlem would never let me live it down if I wasn't involved in her belly casting. Harlem was only in her seventh month, but we messed around and watched a video on belly casting on YouTube while Knight was in New York and she'd been obsessing over it ever since.

When Knight told his father that he wanted him to meet me, he wasn't expecting Princeton to offer to come to his place and try to smooth things out with Harlem, but Knight agreed. I was hoping that worked in my favor. I was hoping we'd do a quick *hi nice to meet ya* then his attention would be on his daughter.

In an attempt to calm my nerves, I went out to the back porch to get some fresh air. Knight was already there. I sat next to him and laid my head on his shoulder, and he wasted no time wrapping his arm around me.

"Knight?"

"Yea, babe?"

"You OK?"

Knight removed his arm from around me, giving me the freedom to turn slightly and face him. His eyes remained forward as he shook his head.

"I just don't want him coming here and messing up the good we got going. It's hard enough keeping her spirits high because of Tage. I don't want him sending her into an even deeper state of sadness."

"Do you think he would really come here and do that? I mean… he basically put her out because she refused to give up her baby. Do you think he would actually come to where she is just to give her a hard time about it?"

"Maybe not intentionally, but he knows what buttons to push, man. His intention might be to come over and try to work things out, but there's no telling what he's going to say in the process. That's what I'm worried about."

"Well, you know you're not going to let him or anyone else hurt her, so it'll work out."

His eyes met mine finally, but they weren't filled with the peace I was hoping for.

"What if it works out too good?"

"What do you mean?"

Knight shrugged and returned his attention to his basketball court.

"What if she goes back with him?"

"You don't want her to?"

He shrugged again and ran his hand over his hair.

"It's not that I don't want her to. I want her to be where she wants to be. It's just... it's been so long since I've had my baby around me like this. And it's my own fault for not being around. It's just... I like her being with me. If she's here I know she's being looked after and well taken care of. I know she's getting the attention she needs. I know she's not getting into anything else she doesn't need to be. This is her home now. She belongs here."

I took his cheek into my hand and ran my thumb across his scruffy beard a few times before turning his face to mine and pecking his lips.

"That is the sweetest thing in life, Knight. I think it's pretty amazing the way you cherish your baby sister. And even though you all have your moments where you butt heads she's just as crazy about you as you are her. She's not going anywhere."

"But it might be best for her to go. When the season starts I'll be gone. Who's going to be here to help her with the baby?"

"Knight, you *know* I'll be here to help her with whatever she needs."

"You already do enough for us, Charlie. You spend more time here than you do your own place. I'm not complaining at all. I prefer it that way. I just would never put that weight on you. Harlem and Hayden are not your responsibility. I appreciate you helping me carry the load, but I don't know. Maybe it'll be best if she left."

Knight stood and walked towards the door, completely shutting down on me. I wasn't used to this with him. He hadn't closed me out emotionally since the first time he tried to kiss me and I ran away.

"So that's it," I asked as I stood, "You're just going to let her go? You know it's better for her and Hayden here, Knight."

He stopped walking but he didn't turn to face me. I walked over to him and placed my hand in the center of his back.

"I get that you're saying this because you think it'll make her leaving easier, but do not go in this house suggesting that she leave just to avoid her not staying. Don't put her out before he even asks her to come back. If you say anything to her about leaving she's going to assume that you don't want her here and she's going to leave. I know it might hurt you if she decides to leave, but let whatever happens happen naturally. Don't bring it up and make the decision for her, Knight."

Losing her. I could see it in his eyes. He was afraid of losing her and Hayden before he even arrived. Knight nodded and grabbed my hand. He pulled me into his chest and kissed my forehead.

"It's times like this when you make me want to make sure you never leave me. Ever."

There was still a trace of darkness in his eyes, but he smiled. That was good enough for now.

"That's what I'm here for."

"Charlie…"

"I'm not leaving you."

This time when he smiled… so did his eyes.

⇗ KNIGHT ⇖

Without Charlie here, this meeting between Harlem, my pops, and I probably would've gone a lot differently, but he hadn't even made it in the house yet and Charlie was already keeping me calm. Yea, he and I resolved a couple of our issues the last time I saw him, Harlem however, was a completely different subject.

I would let no one bring her harm as long as I could protect her from it.

It didn't matter if he was her father or not… I would keep him away from her as well if I had to; especially while she was pregnant.

Charlie's left arm was wrapped around me, and she was using her right hand to caress my stomach. The simple act had my nerves staying in tact as we watched my pops get out of his car and head to the front door. He rang the doorbell but it didn't make me move.

"I should get that," I said, but made no attempt to move.

The doorbell rang again.

Of course Harlem wasn't going to get it.

She hardly ever did.

Unless it was Charlie.

"You need a key," I realized.

She shouldn't have to wait to be let in. She should be able to come and go freely.

"What?" she asked with a smile.

"To the house. You need a key to the house."

I'm sure my announcement seemed random to her, but it was right on time for me. She simply nodded and blushed, so I stepped to the side of her and went to let him in.

We greeted each other casually and he wasted no time walking into the living room searching for Harlem.

He didn't say that's what he was doing or who he was looking for, but the way his countenance fell and shoulders caved at the sight of the empty room said it all.

"She's in her room," I told him as I headed for the kitchen to grab Charlie. She was standing in the same place I'd left her in. "You have no reason to be nervous."

Charlie nodded and reached for my hand. I connected mine with hers, then led her into the living room.

"Harlem," I called. "Pops here."

I watched my father as Charlie and I entered the room. His head tilted and his eyebrows furrowed in confusion, but he quickly smiled and extended his hand for her.

"Pleasure to meet you. Princeton Carver."

"Hi," her voice was its quiet, chipper norm as she smiled. "Charlie White. Pleasure to meet you as well."

Harlem wobbled down the stairs, looking from me to Charlie. Charlie released his hand and took a step towards the stairs.

"Hey, Harlem. How's it going?"

Harlem looked from me to Charlie. Then to him.

"Good."

He nodded and put his hands in his pockets as he rocked on his heels.

"How's the baby? What're you having?"

Harlem looked from me to Charlie. Then to him.

"Good. Boy."

"Wow. My first grandchild. A boy. From my youngest child. Wow."

I opened my mouth to check his ass, but Charlie quickly grabbed my hand and squeezed.

"So do you have a name for him yet?" he continued.

Harlem looked from me to Charlie. Then to him.

"Hayden."

"And the father? Where is he?"

Harlem looked from me to Charlie. But not back to him. Her head lowered as she cupped her hands in the center of her.

"Um, Mr. Carver, why don't you have a seat. Would you like something to eat or drink while you and Harlem catch up?" Charlie interrupted as she grabbed Harlem's hand and sat her down.

I sat next to her as my pops sat in the chair on the opposite side of us.

"Actually, a bottle of water would be nice," he returned his attention to Harlem as Charlie went to get the water. "Listen, Harlem, I know my reaction to you being pregnant may have been a bit... harsh... but I need you to understand where I was coming from."

Charlie handed him the bottle of water and tried to sit on the opposite end of the couch. I don't know who gave her a crazier look between me and Harlem, but she quickly closed the space between us and sat next to Harlem. Her arm went around her on the couch. The feel of her fingers making circles on the back of my neck... it was like she was controlling my emotions with each spin of her fingers. Keeping me in check. I looked down and saw that she was making the same circles on Harlem's thigh with her left hand.

"Harlem," he started regaining my attention. "I was hurt. I was angry. I was disappointed. For the past 10 years I've been a single father, and it has been hard. All I've ever wanted was the best for my children, and you being pregnant at 16 was not the vision I had for your life.

I know that may sound quite selfish of me since it is in fact your life, but as your father... I am you. You are me. What happens in your life happens in mine. The baby that you're carrying is mine. When you told me that you were pregnant I immediately thought about the fact that there would be another child that I'd have to raise without your mother and I just... flipped.

For that, my love, I sincerely apologize. Do you accept my apology?"

Harlem licked her lips and mumbled, "Yes."

"Good. Great. So... what are your plans? Are you working or is the father working? How do you plan on taking care of this baby and finishing school on time?"

"Well... I'm not working right now, but Charlie has been helping me research business ideas. After I have the baby I'm going to work from home after school. That way I won't have to worry about anyone keeping him while I'm at work and school. While I am in school, Princess's aunt is going to keep him.

She has a daycare and she's offered to watch him for me.

No, his father isn't working right now. Tage's father wants his focus to be school and football now, so he gives Tage a monthly stipend. Tage gives half of the money to me when he gets it every month.

I still plan on going to college; even if I have to go online. Knight and Charlie have helped me a lot. They've helped me to see that I can still do all I wanted to do, so I'm confident that I can do this. With God and them of course."

I felt like a proud father. Watching her articulate her plans in such a sure and mature way. I smiled and nudged her shoulder softly. She returned the smile and nudged me back.

"All of that... is great really, but what are you going to do when Knight returns to work? Where are you going to stay? Even if you work from here you will still need help with the baby, Harlem. Especially the first year of his life. And those terrible twos. You'll need help. What are you doing about your living arrangement?"

Harlem scratched her cheek and looked at me briefly.

"Knight said I could stay here."

"Alone? You're 16. You'll be 16 in school trying to work with a newborn. You need help, Harlem. I think it would be best if you came home after the baby was born."

Harlem looked at me again, pleading with me with her eyes to step in, but she needed to make this decision herself.

"It's up to you, sweetheart. Do what's best for you and Hayden. I'll support you either way," I assured her.

"I think..." Harlem looked at Charlie. "I think I should stay here."

His head tilted and he stared at her for a few seconds, but it was a few seconds too long because Harlem lowered her head and inhaled deeply.

"Harlem, I'm really trying to treat you like an adult and give you the space to make this decision on your own... but..."

"I don't want to come home. I don't want to come home. I don't care what I have to do to make it work I'm going to make it work."

"Mr. Carver," Charlie sat up in her seat and look at Harlem and I for permission to speak. "I'm more than willing to help Harlem with whatever she needs while Knight is away."

"And who are you exactly?"

"What you mean who is she?" I asked no longer able to sit and watch in silence. "My woman."

"And my sister," Harlem added as she grabbed Charlie's hand. "She's been helping me this entire time. She has a bedside service for pregnant women. She's been with me every step of the way, Daddy. I don't want to put the pressure on her of having to help me raise my baby, but if she's going to be around because of Knight and she wants to help me I'm going to gladly accept all the help she has to give until I'm capable of doing it on my own."

"What makes you so sure she's going to be around after you have the baby, Harlem? They aren't married. He could cut her off just like he does all the others. She could decide this is too much for her and leave. Then what are you going to do?"

"OK, that's enough. It's clear that you two aren't going to agree on this. So you can leave and maybe try again another day," I cut in as I stood.

He stood and avoided my eyes as he looked at Harlem.

"You're coming home when that baby is born."

"If she wants to stay here she's staying here. I don't care if I have to only announce home games to be here with her and the baby. If this is where she wants to be, this is where she's going to be."

"No, Knight, I would never... no. Please don't do that. It's not that big of a deal. If I have to leave I'll leave, but I'm not letting you do that for me," Harlem stood and grabbed my hand. "You've already done so much. I can't let you do that."

Not wanting to give her father, yea, he was back to being just her father now, the satisfaction of thinking he'd won... I nodded as I looked at him.

"We'll talk about it later. Let me holla at you as you leave, Pops."

He followed me out of my home and I didn't speak until we were at his car.

"What are you doing, man?"

"What do you mean? I'm trying to get my daughter to come home."

"Why? You didn't want anything to do with the baby and now all of a sudden you want them both in your home? Why?"

"It just makes more sense for her to be home, Knight, and you know it. She will need help. She can't do this on her own."

"She will have me and Charlie."

"Here you go with this Charlie shit again..."

"Nah. You can go. I have to let you rule when it comes to Harlem because she's your child and she's 16, but you will not disrespect Charlie in any way. So you can leave before this turns into something that neither of us need it to be."

I walked away and returned to the two most important people in my life.

Charlie

It was my birthday! Dirty 30 and I was ready to get lit! OK, maybe not lit because I couldn't hold my liquor for shit and I was having a rooftop day party, but I was ready to have some fun! I started my day having brunch with my parents and grandparents, then I went to the spa with Veronica. Rodney had to work, so he took me out last night, and Deja was here with me now at my party.

The roof was covered with my closest confidants, and I could honestly feel the love and positivity surrounding me... but there was someone missing. Knight.

Even Harlem's crazy behind snuck up with her best friend after I told her not to because of the drinking that I knew would be going on, but of course she didn't listen to me. She wobbled over to me with her long, beautiful hair blowing in the wind and handed me a gift that I told her not to buy me and kissed me.

Now her and Princess were in the corner of the roof in their own little world.

I spent the night at my own place last night and it felt weird. I felt out of place. Like that wasn't where I belonged. Knight... I'd been craving him since last night. Since I was forced to sleep alone. Since I was forced to deal with the neglect of not having his arms wrapped around me. His breath on the top of my head as he slept. His snores that trailed off as he fell deeper into his sleep. His leg snaking around mine and pulling me closer if I started to move.

I missed my man so freaking much.

So much it scared me.

Making my way over to the bar, I had a glass of wine. I could handle wine. Light sweet wine. It was my second glass and neither had affected me. I stood there and chugged it down as I fought the desire to call Knight. I needed him near me. *Now.*

Deciding on getting close to the closest thing to him here, I started walking towards Harlem, but was stopped and pulled into a chest. A strong chest. My baby's chest. His arm wrapped around my stomach and I couldn't help but smile and moan as he kissed my neck.

"Happy birthday, beauty," he whispered into my neck before kissing it again. "You smell so good, Charlie."

I turned in his embrace and wrapped my arms around his neck. The deep inquisitive look that his eyes naturally held was replaced with a smile as I faced him.

"Where you been? I missed you."

Knight smiled and pecked my lips softly before answering.

"I was taking care of a few things for later today. Say goodbye to all of your friends. You're leaving with me."

"What?" without repeating himself, Knight released me and headed for the exit. "Well, where are we going? I can't leave. It's *my* party, crazy!"

He continued to ignore me as he left the rooftop. With the help of the DJ, I was able to gain everyone's attention at once. After thanking them for coming, I asked Veronica to grab all of my gifts and take them to her home before dashing off the roof, down the stairs, and into Knight's car. Well, I tried to get into Knight's car, but the card, roses, and blue Tiffany&Co box stopped me from sitting down.

I looked into Knight's eyes as mine watered.

"Get in," he ordered.

"I can't," I sniffled as I continued to fight back my tears. "It's stuff there."

Knight chuckled and pulled me back gently. He grabbed everything that was in the seat and stepped back so I could sit down. When I did he put everything in my lap and closed the door. I looked down at everything that he'd placed in my lap as he got in the driver's seat.

"You didn't have to get me anything, Knight. I *told* you and Harlem that."

"Are you gonna open it now, or when we get to the airport?"

"Airport? We're going to the airport? We're going out of town?"

Knight nodded nonchalantly as he stared at me.

"Knight..."

"It's your birthday, Charlie. Did you really expect me to not get you anything or do anything? I have to celebrate you and having you in my life. Read the card and open the box."

My fingers glided over a few of the rose petals before I placed the bouquet on the middle console and picked up the card.

After reading the first line all of the tears that I'd been holding in rushed from my eyes. Like water flowing at the Hoover Dam. This wasn't just a random card he'd pick up. No. He put some thought into this. Like he'd searched through card after card until finding the perfect one. I looked out of the window and shook my head as I inhaled deeply.

"Read the card, Charlie," he pleaded more softly.

I looked over at him and saw in his eyes that maybe he was afraid to say with his mouth how he truly felt. That this card was his way of letting me know in a way that fear couldn't rob either of us of.

With a loud exhale, I read the card from the beginning.

The heart is like a cup. Some new. Some old. Some perfect. Some cracked. All empty and needing to be filled.

On your birthday, I celebrate your life and your heart. And all of the love you've poured into mine.

Happy birthday.

I crawled over the middle compartment into his lap as he laughed.

"Charlie," he laughed more as I kissed him. All over. "Babe, wi-" I cut him off with kisses to his lips. "If you make us miss this flight..."

That returned me to myself. I wanted to travel!

"Thank you, Knight. That was beautiful."

I hugged him and kissed him again before getting back in my seat.

"Now the box. Although you should probably wait. If you had that reaction to the card I'm scared to see how you're going to react to the necklace."

"Knight!"

He laughed as I shoved him in the shoulder.

"What, girl?"

"How are you going to tell me what's in the box? I wanted to be surprised!"

"You taking too long."

"Fine!"

My pout was immediately replaced with a smile as I stared down at the platinum diamond infinity necklace.

"It's beautiful, Knight. Beautiful. Put it on me," turning my back to him, I handed him the necklace so he could put it on me. "Thank you so much, babe. I love it. You're the best boyfriend ever. This is the best birthday ever!"

"There's more. I haven't even gotten started on you yet."

KNIGHT

I took her to Kaupulehu, Hawaii for her birthday. The plan was to stay here for the week. I'd taken care of everything before we left, so all of her clients knew that she was taking a much needed vacation. If they needed anything they were to contact her new assistant Brea.

I expected her to put up a little fight for being away for so long, but she was filled with pure joy when I told her where we were going and for how long. In fact, she didn't think about her clients until we were on the plane headed to Hawaii.

When we arrived, night had fallen, so we spent the night on the beach talking and making love next to the bonfire I started. The next morning, we had breakfast on the patio. It was large and gave us a beautiful view of the ocean and palm trees that she couldn't get enough of. We chilled for a few hours before heading to do some sightseeing and shopping.

After a helicopter ride across the island we returned to our rental to get ready for dinner. To be honest, this restaurant was the reason I chose to bring her here. I found it online and immediately wanted to experience it with her. ULU Ocean Grill and Sushi Lounge was rated as one of the most romantic restaurants, and since I wanted her birthday to be one that she'd never forget… that's where we were going.

Because this was a surprise, I had Deja to pack Charlie's bags. I had no idea what she was wearing tonight for dinner, and as I waited for her I was anxious to see. Charlie was a beautiful woman naturally, but the light and love that was within her shined outwards and made her even more beautiful. She was the most beautiful woman I'd ever encountered in my life. And to this day I still can't believe that she's mine sometimes.

She always listens to music as she gets ready, but the song that she was listening to was replaced with ringing as someone sent her a FaceTime request. Now I wasn't trying to be all up in her business and conversation, but when I heard screaming come out of the phone I had to see what was going on. I had to see what whoever was on the other line was screaming about.

When I made it to the room, Charlie's back was to me as she laughed.

"You good?" I asked gaining her attention.

She turned to face me, and I saw what the screaming was about.

"I'll talk to you later, Day," Charlie said as she ended the call and allowed me to see her.

It was like fate was our DJ and was playing a joke on us because the song that started to play was "Fall for You" by Leela James. Between the lyrics of the song and the monumental moment that was happening before me. Before my very eyes. I was just...

"Here we are together. And everything between us is good. I'm riding this cloud, baby. Ready to fly but before I take another step, would you catch me if I fall for you? Cause I'm falling."

Her strapless dress was white. It stopped just under her knees and hugged every curve she had flawlessly. The dress fit her so well it looked like it was painted on her. Like it was her skin.

"I'm so used to standing. So used to being on my own. But this thing is new, baby. It feels like I'm losing control."

Charlie's face was free of makeup. The only thing on it was what she told me was nude lipstick. I didn't see the point in it since it was practically the same color as her lips, but she liked that shit. And I loved watching her put it on just so I could kiss it off.

"I'll take another step. If you catch me if I fall for you. Cause I'm falling."

Her hair was in its natural curly state. All wild and free how I loved for it to be.

But it was the dress... the dress. The dress is what had Deja calling her and screaming like a maniac. The dress is what had me looking at her speechless. No matter where I looked... my eyes kept returning to the dress.

"Will you promise to be there? Stay by my side always. Whenever I need you don't let me down. If I give you my all don't let me fall. Would you do that for me? Hold me. Will you love me?"

Its deep V neck cut stopped at the top of her navel, exposing the sides of her breasts and the scar going down the center of her chest for all to see. She was showing her scar for the first time in years. Here. With me.

And it was beautiful.

Charlie was beautiful.

Charlie was beauty.

She put her phone on the dresser and pulled one of the roses from her bouquet out. Her smile was small and timid as she walked towards me.

"My heart is ready for love and to be loved. And I choose you, baby. That's the one thing I'm sure of so I will take this one last step. So catch me I'm falling for you."

"This dress..." she started then stopped. "I bought this dress years ago and it's always been a joke between Deja and I because we knew I'd never wear it. Every time we would go out she'd try to make me put it on, but I never would. I'd always take it with me when we traveled just in case I had the confidence to put it on, but I never did."

I looked away from her briefly as she hung her head.

"I know that you brought me here to celebrate my birthday, but I just... I appreciate having you in my life so much, Knight. I haven't worn anything that showed my scar since my surgery, and I honestly don't think I ever would have if it hadn't been for you."

I returned my eyes to her.

"You don't realize the effect you've had on me. Knight, you've done what a real man is supposed to do. You've cultivated me and made me better. Because of the way you cherish me... you've instilled within me confidence and the ability to accept myself.

I know as a woman I have a nasty habit of seeking my validation in men instead of God, and that's what messed me up years ago. I gave a man the power to validate me and make me feel good about myself instead of God. Instead of seeing myself as beautiful and worthy of love and respect.

But it's like... you've reversed what he did to me. The insecurity. The fear. You've taken it away. So I just wanted to thank you for being in my life. Thank you, Knight."

Her arm lifted and she held the rose out for me. Instead of taking it I wrapped my hand around hers and pulled her into me.

"You don't have to thank me for doing what I'm supposed to do, but hearing you voice your appreciation for me... means a lot to me, Charlie. I've never cared enough about a woman to invest in her or see to it that she invested in herself, but you're different. From the beginning I knew you were different. I guess what I'm trying to say is... I love you," she inhaled deeply and the rise of her chest pulled my attention back to the scar.

Back to the proof of me being as good to and for her as she'd been to me and Harlem.

"I'm in love with you, Charlie. I have been for a while but I've been fighting it because it came so hard so fast that I thought it wasn't real, but it is. I love you."

She dropped the rose and pulled me into her. Giving me one of those tight signature Charlie White hugs, but she pulled away quickly.

"I love you," she confessed before hugging me again.

There was something about her not saying, 'I love you too' that struck me to my core. *Too.* Anytime that word was used to convey love it fucked with me. I guess because it meant also. Like… that love was felt or expressed because of the first person who said it. Like… had that first person not expressed or felt it, the second wouldn't have either.

But she didn't say too.

She didn't say also.

She didn't say it like my love for her was the reason she loved me.

No.

She said it like she loved me just to love me. Regardless of if I loved her in return. Like it had been within her just as it was within me and the only reason she hadn't said it was because she was being a true woman. Keeping her feelings on lock and allowing me to initiate while she responded. Keeping power over her heart and making sure that I was committed and on the same level as her before she made that declaration.

She loved me.

Just like I loved her.

"Say it again," I ordered as I carried her over to the bed.

She smiled and sighed as I ran my fingers down the scar. Her hand cupped my cheek, pulling my eyes to hers.

"I love you," she repeated.

Resisting the urge to rip the dress from her body, I pulled it down carefully before doing the same to her panties.

"Again."

She hesitated as she watched me spread her legs and make my way between her thighs.

"I love you."

"Again."

"I…" her nails dug into my shoulders as I showed special attention to her clit. "Love you," she moaned as I slid my finger inside of her.

"Again."

My request fell on deaf ears as her back arched off the bed. The sound of her moaning sounded just as good at this point. I pushed and pulled my finger into her as deep as it could go while sucking her clit. Putting just the right amount of pressure on the top of it to have her coming immediately.

"Charlie..."

"I love you."

I kissed my way up her stomach. Up her scar. Until I made it to her lips. She kissed me hungrily. Sticking her tongue into my mouth like that was where it belonged. It was. I was able to keep myself under control until she bit my bottom lip and stuck her hand in my pants without even unzipping them.

"You want me... don't you?"

"Yes, Knight. Take off your clothes."

Giving in to her request, I stood and undressed completely before sliding back into bed and into her.

"Shit," I groaned – immediately feeling the difference of her with and without a condom.

With a condom she felt amazing. Without a condom she felt life changing. Dangerous. Felt like a trap. The kind of good that had me coming to grips with the fact that I would be a father soon because there was no way in *hell* I was going to pull out of her.

"Don't stop, Knight," she pleaded as she wrapped her legs around me. "Fuck it. Fuck *me*."

With her permission, I buried myself deep inside of her. Trying to make this moment last. Going as slow as I could. Keeping as much control as I could. Between the feel of her cream, her heat, her walls... her nails digging into me as I dug into her... her legs gripping me tightly as she came, then opening widely to let me go deeper... the sound of her moans and heavy breathing... my name falling softly from her lips... there was no coming back at this point.

"Knight," she moaned into my ear as I reached between us to reposition her legs from around my waist to on my shoulders.

I didn't raise up though. I stayed chest to chest with her. Hitting her just as deep. Needing to be just as close. Just as connected. No space. Nothing between us. Nothing could come between us.

"Yes, Charlie," came out more as a moan than an answer.

"I love you," she told me again before my strokes combined with my thumb on her clit made her mute.

"I love you."

I swear I did. And I wasn't afraid to. I wasn't afraid to love her. I wasn't afraid to lose her. I wasn't afraid to feel. There was no way for me to not feel when it came down to her. So I gave in. I felt... and continued to give her something slow, deep, and tender that she could feel.

Charlie

Hawaii made real what I already knew – I loved Knight. I was in love with Knight. And he was in love with me. He loved me. Me. The man was gorgeous. Had lived his dreams, made a profit from it and flipped it, and still had goals and a vision for his life. Financially stable. Natural leader and in tune with the Spirit of God in him. I expected him to be a meanie, but one whiff of my scent had him turning to mush. He could have any woman he wanted and he wanted me. Me!

I was definitely riding cloud nine and wasn't expecting anything to be able to bring me down. Until Harlem called me in tears. Apparently, Tage's father had planted a seed of doubt into him. Now, it wasn't enough for him that Tage didn't have anything to do with her or the baby; he had Tage questioning if the baby was even his!

I tried to explain to her that it wasn't uncommon for a man to ask for a DNA test, but it didn't take long for me to realize she wasn't crying because she was hurt about that. She was crying because she mad. Mad that she'd put herself in the position to have to deal with Tage and his family for the rest of her life.

Five minutes into our conversation she was telling me that her sister was on the other line. When I didn't answer the first call she called her. I told her to just call me back after she finished talking to her, but I decided to go over and see her instead. To cheer her up, I stopped and got her some cookies from Ricki's cookies on the way.

By the time I'd made it to her, she was still on the phone with her sister. I tried to motion for her to not get off the phone, but she didn't listen to me. Carmen hardly ever called either of her siblings. Whenever I was around they always had to call her first. But that was none of my business.

"OK, I'll talk to you later, Carmen. Charlie is here," I couldn't hear what Carmen had said, but she must have asked who Charlie was because Harlem said, "No, Charlie is not a boy, Carmen. She's a woman. Knight's girlfriend. You'd know that if you answered our calls or came home every once in a while."

I always felt awkward being around people when they were having conversations, so I tried to leave her room but she grabbed my wrist and stopped me.

"They've been together for months, Carmen. I don't know. He shouldn't have to text you to tell you something like that. Answer your damn phone! I had to call you three times before you answered! That shit ain't cool! You dan got out there in Atlanta and forgot all about us," Harlem smiled and nodded at whatever Carmen was saying, and just like that her anger had dissolved. "Fine. I know he wanted you to meet her. He said he was just waiting for you to come home again. So this weekend would be perfect. You better come too. Hold on," Harlem looked at me and asked, "Charlie, do you have anything to do Saturday? Carmen says she coming home and wants to meet you."

I shook my head and shrugged. Meeting their sister was even more nerve racking than meeting their father. Because of the strained relationship they had with him, I didn't feel too much of a weight to get him to approve of me. But Carmen… they actually cared about her opinion.

Even though they didn't talk much, she had a way of handling them that no one else could. She had a way of getting them to eat out of the palm of her hand. Like her answering their calls and talking to them for a few minutes at a time was a blessing to them. I was surprised she'd been on the phone with Harlem for as long as she had been. She must not have had anything else to do.

"No. That's… fine," I agree unwillingly.

"Great! If you don't come, Carmen," Carmen cut her threat off and once again said something that made Harlem smile. "Fine. I'll see you then."

Harlem disconnected the call and I suddenly felt unneeded. Not that I was trying to take Carmen's place, but Harlem seemed to be in a better mood because of her sister. Her real sister. Was I jealous? No. Couldn't have been. Maybe possessive was a better word. I hated seeing anyone pull on Harlem's emotional strings; her sister included.

Harlem was like… an egg.

Hard exterior that was meant to protect the softness that was inside, but that hard exterior was way too fragile and easily cracked. She needed to be handled carefully. I understood that. Knight understood that. But Carmen and Princeton… even Tage… they couldn't. Yes, she was outspoken and seemingly rebellious and uncaring, but at the end of the day… she was a little girl. A little girl with a big belly and big responsibility.

She was an egg.

Hard. Fragile. Soft.

KNIGHT

I was on my way home from the gym when Carmen called me. That in itself was a surprise. She didn't call me unless she wanted or needed something or was returning my phone call. But when she told me that she was coming home this weekend I knew something was up. I pulled over onto the side of the road and said...

"Spill it, Carmen. What's going on?"

"What do you mean?"

"Don't bullshit me. I know something is up. What's going on?"

"Just... call me when you get home."

"No. Tell me now."

"But you're driving..."

"I pulled over. What happened?"

She released a hard breath and remained silent until the noise that was around her ceased. She must have gone outside. That was confirmed when I heard a dog barking.

"Harlem called me in hysterics, but when I called back she'd calmed down some because she was talking to a Charlie?"

A smile immediately spread at the sound of Charlie's name.

"Yea. That's mine."

"Since when?"

"Few months ago. Close to four maybe."

"And she's that comfortable with you that she and Harlem are talking?"

It kind of pissed me off that she had the nerve to be calling and asking about Charlie when Charlie was doing all of the shit that she should've been doing with and for Harlem. But whatever.

"Charlie is the one that's been helping Harlem. The girl she was telling you about that we met at Bundled. The one with the bedside service."

"Oh right. Right. The one that works for you. So how did that turn into a relationship?"

"She doesn't work for me, Carmen. She's working with me. Helping me. With *your* baby sister. You need to be thanking her cause you for damn sure haven't shown an interest in helping her with the baby."

"I didn't call you to be reprimanded about not being around."

"Then what did you call for, Carmen?"

Carmen sighed into the phone and what little patience I had was beginning to fade.

"Carmen..."

"There's something you should know about her. I could be wrong. This could be a coincidence. But Charlie isn't a common name for women. Definitely not women in Memphis."

"What are you talking about?"

"I'd feel a lot more comfortable talking about this face to face, or at least when you're home, Knight."

"Cut the bullshit and tell me what you have to tell me."

"All right. All right."

She inhaled deeply and cursed under her breath.

"Knight, you know when mama got really sick towards the end I started going with her to her appointments and emergency room visits because she didn't want daddy to worry about what the doctors were saying?"

I nodded and leaned my head against the headrest.

"Right."

"Well, you remember when I had to take her to the emergency room and we found out that her kidneys were failing and that she needed dialysis?"

"Yea."

"Well... when we were leaving... she saw someone in ICU that made her feel as if God dropped in her spirit that she should help them. She stared at the girl for I don't know how long before the girl's doctor came and asked mama what she needed. Mama went to his office and they talked about what was wrong with the girl. By the end of their conversation mama decided to give the girl her heart when she died."

"What?"

Give her her heart? She was talking about Charlie. She couldn't have been talking about Charlie. Charlie couldn't have had my mother's heart. This had to be a coincidence.

"Mama felt attached to her for some reason. She said she had been looking for a way to find some good coming out of her death, and Charlie was it. Mama ended up meeting with Charlie's parents to get a better understanding of what was going on with her, and after having lunch with them a few times she decided not to do the dialysis and let things happen naturally.

She didn't want any of us to know, just daddy, but because I was there when she first saw Charlie I knew what was going on. She didn't want us to think that she was choosing to die or giving up or nothing like that.

She said that she was trusting God and His plan for her life. And that if His plan was for her to die and give Charlie the chance to live... she found peace in that. That's why it seemed like she'd given up at the end. It wasn't because she didn't want to live anymore; it's just that she'd made up in her mind and heart to trust God and let things happen organically. His way."

I hung up the phone and got back on the road. Carmen called back repeatedly, but I ignored her calls. There was only one person I wanted to talk to about this – Charlie.

Charlie

Harlem and I were in the middle of a SpongeBob marathon when Knight burst into the door and stormed over to us. She was used to this side of him apparently because she hardly flinched. I on the other hand had never seen him this mad. And the fact that his eyes were focused on me had me twice as worried.

With his eyes still locked on me, he said, "Go to your room, sweetheart."

"Go to my room?"

His eyes shifted and he looked at her briefly before returning them to me.

"Now."

Harlem stood and left us alone, and I was kind of sad that she did. I didn't know what the hell was going on, but whatever it was must have been serious to warrant this kind of reaction from him.

Knight's hands went over his mouth as if he was praying, then he ran them down his face as he exhaled loudly.

"I'm going to stay as calm as I possibly can," he assured me, but the coldness in his voice had chills covering my skin. "And I'm only going to ask you this once, so don't lie or play with me, Charlie."

OK.

Now I'm scared.

"Did you know?"

"Did I know what?"

"That you have my mother's heart."

I sat back in my seat. The weight of his words literally knocked the wind out of me. How did he know? Who told him? Why didn't I tell him?

"Knight..."

"Don't. Did you know?"

My head lowered as water filled my eyes. I inhaled deeply as my shoulders caved. I nodded slowly and closed my eyes – trying to prepare for his wrath. When it didn't come I looked up at him. He was looking at the picture he had of her on his wall.

"Knight..."

"Get out."

"What? Knight..."

I tried to grab his hand, but he jerked it away from me.

"Don't fucking touch me. You need to go, Charlie. Now."

Standing, I stumbled over my words nervously.

"Knight... just... if you would let... I didn't know... I mean... I know *now*, but I... didn't... I didn't know *then*."

"Go, Charlie. I swear to God the only thing keeping me from telling you how I really feel is the fact that I love your deceitful ass, but that's about to not mean shit if you don't get out of my face."

"*Deceitful*? How am I deceitful? I didn't know, Knight! I just found out from my doctor right after the auction. After we came back from Vegas I met with him and he told me. I promise I didn't know."

"But you've known for a good two months and didn't think that was something I needed to know?"

There was no way for me to justify keeping this from him, so I didn't try to.

"You need to leave, Charlie."

"But I promised you that I would never leave you."

Dammit.

The tears were falling.

"I don't care about that anymore. You think I care about that now? Now that I know that you're the reason I lost the only woman that..." he put some space between us and inhaled deeply as his fists opened and closed. "She's dead because of you. She died so you could live."

"That's not true. Why would you say that? I... I waited. I waited until she was gone. It wasn't like I *made* her give it to me. Like she was killed so I could have it. It just... happened. They said she was sick."

My mind and everything else around me started spinning. How could he blame me for his mother's death?

"I don't want to hear that shit. Your parents guilted her into not going through with her dialysis trying to save you. Trying to secure a heart for you. Had she not met you she wouldn't have turned the dialysis down. She probably could've lived a little longer. But she saw you and just..."

"You know what? I don't have to stand here and take this. I didn't know then that she was your mother. I didn't know, Knight. I didn't know. And I promise you... if there was a way for me to give her her heart back I would. If there was a way for me to fix this for you I would. But I can't. And I'm sorry. I'm sorry I didn't know. I'm sorry she chose me. I'm sorry *you* chose me. I'm sorry she gave me her heart. I'm sorry I didn't tell you when I found out. I'm sorry. I just didn't want to lose you. But I guess that doesn't matter anymore now."

I grabbed my phone and purse off the couch and headed for the door.

"Charlie, wait."

Thinking he was coming to his senses, I stopped and wiped my tears as I waited for him to make his way to me. When I felt his body heat I turned to face him. Knight snatched the infinity necklace he'd given me from around my neck and I clutched at my heart immediately.

"There is no forever for us, so you don't need this."

My eyes went over his head at Harlem on the bottom stair with tears falling from her eyes.

"I'm sorry," I said to her as I ignored his statement.

I couldn't acknowledge it. I couldn't acknowledge that we were over. Cause I would break. I would fucking *break*. The closer I got to the front door the heavier my heart felt. I heard Harlem in the background yelling for him to go after me, but I didn't want him to. I knew of his pain. His anger. His guilt. His love for his mother.

I never wanted to be a part of that. I wanted to give him love. And peace. And happiness. Not this. Not a reminder of the thing he valued most and lost. Not death.

I didn't want him to come after me. And quite frankly, I didn't want Angela's heart anymore. She wasn't mine anymore. She was his. And now... I wasn't.

⋗ KNIGHT ⋖

"You're lucky I'm pregnant, otherwise I'd beat your ass!" Harlem yelled as she smacked the back of my head.

It didn't register. Nothing was. Nothing could hurt me more than the thought of the woman I love keeping this from me. I knew I didn't think rationally when I was angry, that's why I told her to leave. But she just *had* to stay. She just had to stay and try to make me understand.

I walked out to my car with Harlem still going off behind me. Charlie said she didn't know, and I wanted to believe her. I wanted to believe that this was... some miracle. Some twisted miracle. That somehow my mother had given me one final gift... the best gift she could've ever given me. Charlie.

I tried to tell myself that without my mother's heart Charlie might've died and I wouldn't have had either of them, but that wasn't making me feel better at this point.

I needed to talk to my father.

I needed him to make this make sense.

"You better be going to apologize!"

"Take your ass back in the house. Walking around out here with no shoes on," I grumbled while getting in my car.

She stood there with her arms crossed over her chest until I backed out of the driveway.

The entire ride to my pops house Charlie's face kept popping into my brain. Her tears. The fearful look in her eyes. The way it looked like she literally stopped breathing when I took the necklace from her.

I didn't mean to do that shit. I mean... I meant to do it, but I didn't mean to do it. I didn't mean to break up with her. I didn't mean to yell at her. She should've just left and given me time to process this shit like I asked.

But that was Charlie. Staying like she said she always would.

After cutting my car off I called her and she sent me to voicemail. I called again and she sent me to voicemail.

As I got out of the car I shot her a text.

I'm sorry. Let me apologize.

Normally I'd knock and let pops let me in, but I didn't have time to wait today. I used my key and let myself inside.

"Pops!"

"In the kitchen."

I found him in the kitchen sitting at the table with a cup of coffee and his newspaper like it wasn't the middle of the day.

"Why didn't you tell me? You knew Charlie when you saw her. That's why you looked at her the way you did. Why didn't you tell me she had mama's heart?"

He folded the newspaper, placed it on the table, and took a sip of his coffee before he answered.

"Because I knew you'd break up with her, and that that would be the biggest mistake of your life."

I ran my hand over my head as he motioned for me to sit in the seat across from him.

"Explain everything. Start from the beginning."

He went on to give me the expanded version of what Carmen told me earlier. That my mother did see Charlie while Charlie was in her hospital bed, and immediately felt something for her. A pull towards her. She spoke with Charlie's doctor and found out that her heart was failing her. That she'd spent years in and out of the emergency room because of heart complications.

How she'd gone through all possible treatments with her heart specialist, and all she could do was wait for a heart.

He said that my mother immediately had the desire to give Charlie her heart, and when he tried to talk her out of it she just straight up refused. She convinced him that her heart wouldn't be of any use for her when she was gone, and that eventually she was going to die anyway.

She reached out to Charlie's parents and spoke with them about Charlie on numerous occasions. Charlie didn't know about anything that was going on because they weren't sure how long my mother had and they didn't want to get her hopes up. As much as they wanted a heart for her, they pleaded with my mother to do the dialysis, but she didn't.

She told them and my father that she'd prayed and knew that her kidneys failing wouldn't be the reason she died. She was filled with such peace and happiness at the thought of giving Charlie her heart that she didn't care what happened to her up until that point.

As she said, her kidneys failing weren't the reason she died. The dialysis may have made her last days more pleasant, but it wasn't necessary. It wouldn't have stopped her from having a stroke. It wouldn't have stopped her from laying in the bathroom so long without medical attention that she was brain dead by the time my father found her.

And what made it even more of something that was meant to be was the fact that Charlie died at the same time my mother did, but because of my mother's heart... Charlie lived.

She lived.

And she was here with me.

And not only was she here with me, but my mother was too. *Too*. Also. Along with Charlie. Too fit perfectly here. Perfectly.

Because of her heart.

Charlie had my mother's heart inside of her.

It wasn't a bad thing.

It was a good thing.

It was a miracle.

It was how she made sure that even after she was gone that she'd still be here with us.

If I haven't ruined my chance of having Charlie. Of having them both.

"Thanks for telling me," I mumbled as I stood – feeling like total and complete shit.

I shouldn't have rushed home to confront her. I should've come here first or waited until I cooled down.

"No problem, son. I'm sorry I didn't tell you before. I should have told you when I saw her, but I didn't want you to react irrationally. I was hoping that you'd grow to love her enough to overlook the fact that we kept this from you. That you wouldn't punish her or yourself because of the decision your mother made."

I nodded as I made my way out of the kitchen.

Too late for that.

Charlie

I couldn't go to my apartment. It would be empty and make me want to be at my real home. My home with Knight and Harlem. So I busied myself checking on my clients until the sun went down. Trying not to think about Knight. About Harlem. About Angela.

He called me a few times. Sent a few text messages. He even sent me three emails. I didn't respond to any of it. Yes, I knew he was lashing out in anger, but that didn't stop the hurt. That didn't keep me from crying every time one of my clients asked me how I was doing. Every time I went to the bathroom. Every time I was in my car alone.

By the time I pulled up to my apartment I thought I'd be all cried out by now, but the sight of Knight sitting on my doorstep had tears puddling up in my eyes. Not wanting to be further yelled at for something that was out of my control, I started my car up again. As I reversed he stood and jogged over to my car.

I tried to pull out. I wanted to pull out. But I couldn't. I couldn't leave him. I promised I'd never leave him. With that draining revelation I pulled back into my parking space and cut my car off. Before I could even get my seatbelt off good Knight was opening the door and pulling me out of it.

"I'm so sorry," he apologized as he pulled me into his chest.

I couldn't hug him back right away. Still hurt too much. But I did apologize for my part in this.

"I'm sorry for not telling you as soon as I found out."

"You're not gonna hug me back?"

That made the tears fall.

"You hurt my feelings, Knight."

"I know, babe, and I'm *so* sorry. I was just angry and I know that's not a good excuse, but when I get mad I can't think straight," he released me only to look into my eyes. "I love you, Charlie. I don't want to lose you."

"But you said..."

"Forget what I said. Forget it all. All that matters to me is that I have you. It fucked with me at first I'm not going to lie, but the calmer I got the more I was able to think clearly," his palms went to my cheeks as he stared into my eyes. "You having my mother's heart is a blessing."

I tried to hang my head but he lifted it.

"Not only do I have you... this amazing, beautiful, sweet, loving woman... but I have my mama too. In you. You're loving me with her heart, Charlie. I haven't been able to let any other woman in because my heart has been reserved for you. No one else could complement me the way you do. I don't know if she knew that you were the one for me, or if God put her up to this because He knew that we'd get to this point eventually... but I'm happy, Charlie. I'm happy that you have her heart. It wouldn't... this wouldn't... *we* wouldn't be the same if you had anyone else's. I'm not saying that having her heart is what made me love you... but you having her heart... just solidifies that you're the one for me."

Taking his hands into mine, I used them to pull him closer to me.

"When you first told me about your heart condition I went to my pops and asked him how he handled losing my mama. I asked him how to prepare to lose you. I don't ever want to lose you, Charlie. God chose you. My mother chose you. I chose you. I *choose* you. I don't want anything to pull you from me but death, and I'm hoping I die first in like 80 years."

I smiled for the first time in hours as the heaviness that was in my heart when I left him earlier started to fade away.

"He told me a lot that day, but the thing that sticks out the most right now was that when I realized I couldn't live without you... not to."

Knight released my hand and pulled a box out of his pocket. He took a small step back before getting down on one knee.

"Knight..."

"I can't. I can't live without you. I don't *want* to live without you. I *need* you, Charlie. You make me feel. I need to feel. I love you so much and I'm so sorry for making you doubt that earlier," he opened the box and I swear my knees buckled when he pulled that ring out. "I want you, Charlie. For life. Will you marry me?"

It crossed my mind to make him sweat. To tease him a little. Take a long time to answer or not answer at all. But as I looked down into those eyes... those beautiful deep, dark, inquisitive eyes... I felt like this had always been the question. This had always been the question behind his eyes. The question of if I would ever leave him. If I would always be here. And there was no way I could deny him of that any longer.

"You know I will. *Yes*," my lips trembled as I fought my tears but fuck it.

I let them fall anyway.

Knight slid the ring onto my finger, and to my surprise, it was the perfect fit. He stood and pulled me into him but kept from kissing me.

"I have something else that belongs to you," he said as he reached into his pocket again.

I looked down as his hand came out of his pocket clutching my forever with him. My necklace. Turning, I allowed him to put the necklace on me. I grabbed it and ran my fingers across it as I turned to face him. His lips were on mine at the same time that he pulled me into his arms. And as usual... it was in his chest that I found peace.

"I love you," he whispered into my lips before kissing me again.

"I love you. Let's go home."

Harlem

This day didn't come as a surprise to anyone. Seven months after what could have split them up forever, Knight and Charlie were getting married. What did surprise me, however, was the little baby growing inside of Charlie's stomach. It was crazy how Hayden, who was only two months old, would be older than their child! Every time I think about that I smile.

Charlie was the most gorgeous bride I'd ever seen. Her soft chiffon off the shoulder wedding dress displayed her baby bump beautifully. She was glowing and her light had everyone around her smiling.

Especially Knight.

He had the brightest smile on his face as they swayed across the dancefloor during their first dance as husband and wife. Every so often he'd rub her belly and whisper something in her ear that would make her smile and grip his shoulder.

I was happy for my big brother. Happy that he'd finally let her in. Let love in. Allowed himself to feel. Removed the numbing pain and guilt and hurt that had been consuming him for years.

This was just the beginning for them, and I couldn't wait to watch their love unfold.

Don't worry, you'll have your chance to watch too... but in me, Hayden, and Tage's story, though.

Until then...

THE END.

Thank you so much for reading! I'd really appreciate it if you left a review and recommended this book to your friends if you enjoyed it!

Let's connect!

Author Page - www.facebook.com/authorblove
Instagram – www.instagram.com/authorblove
Twitter – www.twitter.com/authorblove
Website – www.authorblove.com
Paperback books – www.blovesbooks.com
Self-love classes! - http://blove.teachable.com

Help Us Solve
The Cruel Mystery

LUPUS™
FOUNDATION OF AMERICA

WE NEED
YOUR USEABLE CLOTHING

Lupus is an unpredictable and misunderstood autoimmune disease that affects an estimated 1.5 million Americans. There is no cure and we need your help today to find one!

(OVER)

WE HAVE A
TRUCK COMING TO
YOUR STREET!

PICK-UP DATE:

Tuesday, June 27

PLEASE CALL NOW
1-(888) 445-8787 OR
SCHEDULE AT WWW.LUPUSPICKUP.ORG

Lupus Foundation of America, Inc.
2121 K Street N.W. Suite 200
Washington, DC 20037

19-20608***************ECRWSS**C021
019-0602F-0627
RESIDENT
57 UNION ST APT 22
MONTCLAIR, NJ 07042-3334

Why Donate to the Lupus Foundation of America?

The Lupus Foundation of America is the only national force devoted to solving the cruel mystery of lupus while giving caring support to those who suffer from its brutal impact. Through our programs of research, education and advocacy, we lead the fight to improve the quality of life for all people affected by lupus.

Lupus is a Cruel Mystery!

Lupus is hidden from view and undefined, has a range of symptoms, and strikes without warning. It has no known cause and no known cure. Lupus is debilitating and destructive and can be fatal, yet research on lupus remains underfunded relative to its scope and devastation.

Help Us Solve the Cruel Mystery!

Your contribution of clothing, shoes and household goods helps fund our programs. We sell your donated goods to private companies by annual bid and use the proceeds to realize our vision of a life free from lupus.

Join the Fight!

For more information about lupus or the urgent work of the Lupus Foundation of America, visit our website at lupus.org.

Lupus can affect any organ, and a wide range of symptoms can occur. These symptoms may come and go, and different symptoms may appear at different times during the course of the disease.

Common symptoms of lupus:

- Extreme fatigue (tiredness)
- Butterfly-shaped rash across cheeks and nose
  - Joint pain
  - Sun-sensitivity
  - Kidney problems

Listen to your body, track your symptoms and talk to your doctor. Early diagnosis and treatment may help to prevent or lessen serious health consequences of lupus.

You do not need to be home. Driver will leave a donation receipt.

Help Us Solve
The Cruel Mystery
LUPUS
FOUNDATION OF AMERICA

WHAT TO DONATE:

- CLOTHING -
  All types & sizes
- SHOES -
  All types & sizes
- ALL BEDDING ITEMS
- DRAPERIES & CURTAINS
- HOUSEWARES & GLASSWARE
- JEWELRY
- TOYS & GAMES
- KNICK KNACKS
- SMALL APPLIANCES
- TOOLS - All kinds

HOW TO DONATE:

- Schedule a truck to stop by your home on the designated day.
- Place donated items on your porch or another location that can be seen by the driver by 7:30AM on the scheduled day (rain or shine).
- Attach this postcard to identify your donation or clearly mark your bags or boxes "LFA."
- The driver will leave a tax receipt.
- If this postcard arrives too late, or the time we specified is inconvenient, please call **1-888-445-8787** or go online to **www.lupuspickup.org** prior to the scheduled pickup date to arrange for another pickup date.

THANK YOU!

NEW JERSEY: INFORMATION FILED WITH THE ATTORNEY GENERAL CONCERNING THIS CHARITABLE SOLICITATION AND THE PERCENTAGE OF CONTRIBUTIONS RECEIVED BY THE CHARITY DURING THE LAST REPORTING PERIOD THAT WERE DEDICATED TO THE CHARITABLE PURPOSE MAY BE OBTAINED FROM THE ATTORNEY GENERAL OF THE STATE OF NEW JERSEY BY CALLING (973) 504-6215

AND IS AVAILABLE ON THE INTERNET AT HTTP://WWW.STATE.NJ.US/LPS/CA/CHARFRM.HTM. REGISTRATION WITH THE ATTORNEY GENERAL DOES NOT IMPLY ENDORSEMENT.

NEW YORK: Upon request, a copy of the last financial report may be obtained from the LFA, 2121K Street, N.W., Suite 200, Washington, DC 20037 or from the Attorney General Charities Bureau, 120 Broadway, New York, NY 10271.

LFA-LI/NJ

Made in the USA
Columbia, SC
25 May 2017